M, T.

AN UNSUITABLE ALLIANCE

Averil Townley, whose life is dominated by her overbearing father, is captivated by the exploits of the Suffragettes and their fight for women's rights. The advent of James Rushworth into her life brings a hitherto unknown delight; but, when her fortunes take a downward turn and James melts away, Averil fears it is because he no longer sees her as a suitable match. Undeterred, Averil determines to take control of her own destiny . . . but will that destiny include James?

KAREN ABBOTT

AN UNSUITABLE ALLIANCE

Complete and Unabridged

LINFORD
Leicester

First published in Great Britain in 2005

First Linford Edition
published 2006

British Library CIP Data

Abbott, Karen
  An unsuitable alliance.—Large print ed.—
Linford romance library
  1. Love stories
  2. Large type books
  I. Title
  823.9'14 [F]

  ISBN 1–84617–299–3

Published by
F. A. Thorpe (Publishing)
Anstey, Leicestershire

Set by Words & Graphics Ltd.
Anstey, Leicestershire
Printed and bound in Great Britain by
T. J. International Ltd., Padstow, Cornwall

This book is printed on acid-free paper

1

Nineteen-year-old Averil Townley drew in her breath sharply as her eyes hastily scanned the news item on the front page of last night's Bolton Evening News. Emily Davison, a militant suffragette, had flung herself in front of the King's horse at the Derby the previous day. Emily and the jockey had sustained serious injuries, the horse more moderately so.

Oh, how brave of the young woman! Averil wished she were only half as brave.

A series of, 'Hush!' and sharp sounds of, 'Ssh!' rippled around the reading room in of Horwich Library.

Averil felt her cheeks redden, though she was determined not to be intimidated by the other occupants of the room — all male, she noted derisively. Hiding her derision, she made herself

1

smile brightly at each elderly man in turn and had the satisfaction of seeing their sharp expressions overtaken by a mixture of embarrassment and discomfiture.

Averil returned her gaze to the newspaper and read further details of the severity of Emily's injuries, which somewhat deflated the surge of suffragist fervour that had coursed through her body. She sighed deeply, torn between admiring the outrageous incidents that had filled the newspapers over the past few years and regretting the necessity that had persuaded the women involved in the suffragette movement to commit offences.

If only the politicians would listen to the grievances of the unenfranchised, the women wouldn't have to gain their attention by these other means.

Without thinking, Averil brought her clenched fist down firmly upon the table. Her action brought more sounds of annoyance from the other readers. An elderly bewhiskered gentleman laid down his newspaper and rose to his feet, glowering at Averil.

'Young lady! Will you be so courteous as to either remain silent or remove yourself from this quiet room?' he hissed. 'Or shall I resort to calling the librarian and asking him to remove you?'

A murmur of approval circulated around the small room, and for the second time Averil felt her cheeks warm. She straightened her shoulders and rose to her feet with a slight toss of her head. A few stray tendrils of her chestnut curls had escaped from the pins that gathered the rest of her coiffure just below the crown of her head, framing her face.

Her lips were set in what her elderly father would call her 'mulish' look and, as she swept from the reading room, she managed to tilt her head with a touch of arrogance that she was far from feeling.

To Averil's relief, Mr Perkins, the chief librarian, was occupied elsewhere and one of his female assistants was on duty at the desk. Averil had heard her speak at a meeting of the local National Union of Women's Suffrage Societies and knew her to be called Rosie Hardshaw.

Rosie's eyebrow rose fractionally as Averil swept indignantly towards her.

'Men!' Averil said, scathingly.

Rosie smiled sympathetically. She hadn't heard the short confrontation in the reading room but, from Averil's demeanour, she could imagine its nature.

'Did you upset them?' she asked.

Averil grimaced. 'I'm afraid so!'

She dropped the folded newspaper on to the desk. 'I was reading about Emily Davison,' she breathed fervently, clasping her hands at her breast. 'What a brave young lady.'

'A tragic figure.' Rosie agreed. 'Though I doubt the wisdom of her action.'

Averil was taken aback. 'But she was willing to risk her life for the cause.'

'And put another to risk. Not to

mention the poor horse.'

'Yes, well . . . ' Averil floundered. She hadn't expected her views to be challenged by another 'sister' to the cause, however gently expressed.

Rosie smiled at her confusion. 'You will come across many differing views amongst our sisterhood, Averil. You must be prepared to weigh each one by your own conscience.'

'Y . . . yes,' Averil slowly agreed. She silently considered Rosie's words, feeling slightly rebellious against the caution expressed . . . though she was honest enough to recognise that Rosie wasn't censuring her by pointing out that others might not agree wholeheartedly with every suffragette action.

'But you went to prison to further the cause!' she burst out impulsively.

'Did everyone agree with that?'

Rosie laughed. 'No,' she admitted, 'but it felt like the right thing to do at the time.'

She reached out and laid a gentle hand on Averil's arm. 'Whatever you do, Averil, don't lose your enthusiasm. We need eager young ladies like you.' She glanced at the wall clock. 'Anyway, hadn't you better be going? It's almost dinnertime and . . . '

Averil's hands flew to her face as she followed Rosie's glance.

'Oh, good heavens! Is that the time? You're right, Mrs Hardshaw! Oh, dear. Father will . . . ' She began to rush towards the door. 'Goodbye, Mrs Hardshaw. I'll see you tomorrow.'

'Call me Rosie!'

Averil acknowledged the call with a wave of her hand and hurried down the library steps into Jones Street.

Her high-heeled boots sounded their fast tattoo against the paving as she hastened down to Lee Lane, where most of the shops were situated, and turned to the left. If she hurried, she might reach home before her father was aware of her late arrival.

Even as she ran, she sighed in exasperation with herself for being so unaware of the passing time. A sense almost of dread settled deep in her heart. Unpunctuality was a sin too severe to be readily forgiven in Joshua Townley's eyes. He abhorred it with every atom of his being and had instilled his abhorrence of it into his only child's upbringing.

Not that Averil felt it to be so great a matter of concern. Indeed, its keeping was as much an abhorrence to her as its neglect was to her father and she had suffered any number of reprimands and punishments throughout her life so far . . . and would probably continue to do so in the years ahead, she ruefully reflected.

But the suffrage cause had grasped at her lively mind and she felt a great affinity to the claims of the many women who had lately awoken to the realisation that women were deprived of their rightful place in society by the laws of their land. The injustice of it all tore at Averil's heart, for didn't she suffer from male domination herself? If only she had been born a boy, how

7

different her life would have been.

She would have been allowed to stay on at school and to go to university. If that had been unattainable, though Averil avowed that that would not have been the case, she would also have been given an allowance to spend as she desired and would have had the promise of some form of employment to look forward to.

She would have been able, at the right time of her life, to own property and dispose of it as she wished and, most important of all, she would have had the right to vote in political elections and have some say in the way that the laws of the land were made.

Averil's face was pink with exertion and the wrestling of her inner thoughts as she hurried beyond the top of Winter Hey Lane. Here, where Lee Lane became Church Road, the gradient became steeper as the road began to rise to where the parish church was sited overlooking the town.

It was a lovely June day and the sun

was shining brightly in the clear blue sky. A few small clouds trailed lazily across the sky but Averil didn't notice them as she hurried up the hill and past the church.

What excuse could she give, except that she had been so engrossed in her reading that she had been unaware of how late it was? In Joshua's opinion, young ladies did not parade themselves in public in male-dominated pursuits . . . nor did they handle books and newspapers that had been previously mauled by the general, unwashed public.

'Do you know how many dirty fingers have pawed through the pages of those books?' he had angrily demanded on more than one such occasion when Averil's attendance at the library had unfortunately reached his notice. 'Wash your hands immediately before you touch anything in this house.'

In vain did she beg permission to read his newspapers . . . after he had read them, of course. In his opinion, his newspapers were too 'highbrow' for young ladies. She would not understand what she was reading.

So furious were her thoughts, that she strode off the edge of the paving and into the roadway without first stopping to make sure that the road was clear.

The honk of a motorcar penetrated her mind, and for a frozen second or two, she stared in horror at the vehicle that was about to mow her down.

Her mind leapt unasked into her earlier thoughts of the splendid horror of Emily Davison's act as she flung herself under the hooves of the King's horse . . . but there was no splendour here. Only a vivid stab of fear. She was about to die.

She registered the shock on the driver's face followed by the contortions of anger, fright and determination as he strove to evade the almost inevitable collision.

With a screech of brakes, the burning smell of rubber on the cobblestones and the lurching forward of the driver, the vehicle slammed to a standstill less than a foot away from her petrified body as abruptly as if it had been driven into a stone wall.

Averil's eyes were wide with shock. Both of her hands had risen to shoulder height, ready, it seemed, to ward off the force of the impact of the motorcar. Now that that danger was past, her fingers spread across her cheeks and she stared wordlessly as the irate driver leaped down from his seat and advanced upon her.

'Damn you, woman! Are you wanting to kill yourself?' he shouted at her.

His anger swiftly brought her mind out of its suspension from life and fanned the remnants of her fright into flames of fury.

'How dare you speak to me in such a manner? You nearly killed me with your reckless driving!' she vehemently retorted. 'Springing out of nowhere, like that! And you were driving far too fast.'

She made an exaggerated show of looking around. 'Are you in a race or something? Where are all the others? Don't tell me you are coming in last.'

The young man folded his arms and tapped his right foot on the ground. He raised a sardonic eyebrow.

Refusing to be deterred, Averil continued, 'And aren't you supposed to sound your horn when you approach pedestrians?'

The man glared down at her, his clenched fists now upon his hips. 'I did sound my horn,' he replied coldly, obviously putting some firm restrain on his tongue. 'You, apparently, chose not to hear it. And, as for driving too fast, are you not aware that, coming up a hill as steep as this one, my vehicle can do no more than fifteen miles an hour.'

'Well, that's at least five times faster than I can walk.' Averil declared, with scant regard for the mathematical truth. 'Probably ten times faster up this hill.'

Her fright was calming and she found herself appraising the young man. He was tall and good-looking, some few years older than her, about twenty-four or five years of age, she reckoned. His dark brown hair was fashionably short, well-trimmed at the back and sides and his face was clean-shaven, revealing a fascinating dimple at the corner of his mouth. His features were strong. The knowledge that he was not a man to tangle with too lightly, flitted through her mind . . . though she instantly erased the insight.

The turbulence of her thoughts concerning her grievances against her father now sought a different target, one more to hand, a target right in front of her.

Unconsciously aping her adversary's pose, she tucked the backs of her hands on to her hips but, for once in her life, Averil now found herself to be speechless.

Her mind seemed to be spinning uncontrollably and, although she tried to pull it back into control, she found it very difficult, since her eyes kept wandering to his now slightly smiling mouth. She wondered if his lips were as soft and velvety as they seemed, and if she were to twist that small curl of dark brown hair that hung over his forehead around her finger, would it spring back into its place when she let it go? She swallowed hard.

If the truth be known, she suddenly felt as though she had been struck in her midriff and that her heart was turning rapid somersaults within her. Time stood still and, although she knew that some response would soon be demanded of her, she felt unable to speak further. Confused, she broke contact with his eyes and glanced down.

As her long dark lashes momentarily covered her eyes, the man, James Rushworth noticed the spray of golden freckles that delicately covered the bridge of her delightfully small nose and spread out on to her cheeks. An irresistible urge to touch them caused his right hand to rise of its own volition and it took a determined self-denial to prevent the far-too-personal gesture.

Even so, he was unprepared for the bolt as she raised her eyelashes again and gazed at him with eyes of startling clarity. He raised his hand again, as though to take off his hat, remembering too late that he was not wearing one. He gave a short laugh to cover his embarrassment and held out his hand.

'James Rushworth,' he introduced himself.

Her facial reaction was one of confused indecision. He thought that she looked absolutely delightful. Her pink cheeks heightened the brightness of her dark brown eyes and her deliciously pink lips were fixed in an 'Oh!' of surprise, as she too extended her hand.

'How ... how do you do ... er ... Mr Rushworth?'

James took hold of her hand. 'And you are?'

'Averil Townley ... Miss,' she added unnecessarily.

Of course she was 'Miss'. She was far too young to be married. The thought that she might be married hadn't even occurred to him . . . though, as she amended her status, he had felt a surge of delight run through him.

They stood and smiled at each other, their initial annoyance with each other forgotten. It was James who eventually brought his senses together and shook his mind clear.

'I am pleased to have met you, Miss Townley.'

Though still holding her hand, he dragged his eyes away from her face and looked up and down the road, seeking inspiration for what to say next. 'May I drive you home?' he asked hopefully.

A smile of delight lit Averil's face. It instantly made him think she was going to say, 'yes', but the ready response on her lips instantly faded and her eyes betrayed her urgent need to be on her way.

'Thank you, but no! No, that wouldn't do at all. Father wouldn't like it.'

Even though he understood, her words seemed to cut through him like a knife. It was a new experience for him, and he wasn't sure he liked it.

Averil pulled her hand out of its captivity and backed away. With visible effort, it seemed, she pulled her thoughts together and, when she spoke again, it was with determination.

'Goodbye, Mr Rushworth. Thank you. I must go.'

'James. Please call me James.'

Once more, she dragged her eyes away from his and glanced hastily up and down the road. Then, with a flurry of her blue skirt, she hurried across the road to the opposite side and she hurried up the hill without so much as a backward glance.

2

Averil hurried up the hill as quickly as she could. Her mind was in turmoil. How could her life change so much in such a short time?

Starting from five short minutes ago, her life was now spinning on a different axis. And at its centre was a handsome young man named James Rushworth.

She was surprised at the reaction she had caused in him . . . for her feminine intuition, untutored though it might be, had recognised the masculine instinct in James' bearing. He had liked her. She was certain of it. And she liked him.

Even so, she was conscious of trouble ahead. She knew her father would be angry at her lateness and would, no doubt, shout angrily at her mother as much as at herself.

The wrought iron gate clanged back

into its place as she swirled up the front path to the family home. It was a double-fronted, three-storeys-high, detached house, standing in its own garden, back, front and to the sides.

The flower gardens at the front and sides of the house were a credit to the skill and dedication of Fred Hesketh, their gardener.

As a last minute change of plan, Averil swerved away from the front steps, their edges donkey-stoned every morning by Mary Ellen, their scullery maid, and hastened past the window of their sitting room, where, no doubt, her mother would be seated, anxiously awaiting her late arrival. She hurried round the side of the house to the rear entrance and unceremoniously whirled into the kitchen.

'Eh, Miss Averil, wherever have you been? Your father's been ranting and raving since the clock struck twelve!' Hannah Hesketh, their housekeeper remonstrated. Her astute eyes took in Averil's pink face and her dishevelled

19

hair as she stood getting back her breath by the well-scrubbed kitchen table.

'Is everything all right, Miss Averil? Your mother's all of a-dither and t'master isn't fit to be heard by any good-livin' Christian folk!'

'Oh, dear. I'm sorry, Mrs Hesketh,' Averil hastily apologised, the fingers of her right hand splayed across the front of her chest. 'And you, Mary Ellen. Yes, I'm fine, just a little out of breath. I forgot the time. Be a dear, Mary Ellen and fetch me a comb whilst I wash my hands and face at the sink. Maybe Father won't be too angry if I make myself look respectable again. Is dinner ready, Mrs Hesketh?'

'Eh, I'm sorry, Miss Averil, but I've had to serve it long since, he were in that much of a state.'

'In a state' was probably the under-statement of the year, Averil thought ruefully, knowing her father's insistence on meals being served promptly at the correct time and everything arranged in accordance with the finite details of his instructions. How long would it be before his wrath descended upon her?

Strangely, it occurred to her that she didn't feel quite the same level of apprehension as she normally did in such instances. The latent excitement of her meeting with James Rushworth was still making her feel slightly lightheaded and almost giddy. She had better sober her emotions before she met with either of her parents.

However, even as she turned from the sink, she saw the kitchen's inner door open and her mother stepped into the room. Although only in her mid-fifties, Grace Townley looked much older and her once dark chestnut hair was completely white.

After many childless years she had conceived Averil in her mid-thirties and, following the difficult pregnancy and even more difficult birth, she had been warned by the family doctor not to attempt to have any more babies, much to her husband's displeasure. He had hoped for a son . . . and had never forgiven either of the two women in his life.

Averil felt sorry for her mother, caught as she was between a stern, unforgiving husband and, in Joshua's words, her 'flighty and wilful' daughter. Maybe she was flighty and wilful, Averil reflected wryly.

Grace's anxiety made her face look strained and her voice shook as she spoke. 'Averil, there you are at last! Oh, how could you be so late?' She wrung her hands nervously. 'Your father wants to see you immediately in his study.'

Her face softened a little as she touched Averil lightly on the arm. 'Don't antagonise him any further, will you, dear.

'I wish to call upon Cissie Pilling this afternoon to talk about the opening of the Operatic Society, and I hoped you might accompany me. You have quite a sweet voice, you know, Averil.'

For a moment of two, Grace's face relaxed a little and remnants of her former beauty shone through her now much-lined face, as she looked lovingly at her daughter.

Averil felt a rush of love mixed with pity for her mother and smiled more brightly than she felt. 'That's all right, Mother. I'll still be able to come. It won't take me long to change and redo my hair. I don't mind about not having any lunch, honestly.'

'No, no. You don't understand. Your father has now forbidden it as a punishment for being late, and he will be angrier than ever if you don't come immediately.'

Averil's face fell. It was true that she didn't feel hungry — the excitement of her encounter with James Rushworth had seen to that — and she had too many memories of her father's severity to contemplate lightly another clash with him.

A surge of rebellion flowed through her and, as she passed the kitchen table, she reached out and plucked two large strawberries from a bowl of the delicious fruits.

'Then I shall eat these!' she said lightly. 'For I truly believe that I have not done anything so bad as to merit the punishment of starvation.'

She popped the succulent fruits into her mouth and, with an attitude of light-heartedness that went no deeper than her outer being, she swept past her mother through the inner door of the kitchen into the rear of their house and crossed the hall to the door of Joshua Townley's study.

With her mother's faint cry of, 'Oh, Averil! Take heed!' ringing in her ears, she knocked imperiously on the door and, barely waiting for the terse command of, 'enter!' she opened the door and stepped inside the sombre room.

Joshua Townley, when in his prime, had been, in the universal opinion of his former work colleagues and underlings, a man to be feared and rarely to be crossed. He ruled his home with the same severity and looked upon any lessening of such to be a show of weakness . . . a trait of character that he abhorred and despised. Blind obedience and respect for his authority, he demanded as his right.

His hair, formerly as black as the coal that lay underground in the surrounding Lancashire coalfields, was now iron-grey. His equally grey moustache and neatly trimmed beard barely disguised his hard, thin lips. He had been a tall man but the crippling condition of arthritis had, in recent years, ravaged his former upright and slender figure and now, his shoulders were stooped as he stood by the sash window staring out into the rear garden of his home.

He didn't turn to greet his daughter and it was Averil who eventually broke the silence that stretched between them.

'You wanted to see me, Father?'

'I wanted to see you more than an hour ago.' Joshua said sharply. His eyes narrowed as he took in her dishevelled hair and pink cheeks.

'How dare you come home in such a state? You look like common trollop. I won't have you besmirching our name in this way. Do you hear me? Where have you been?'

'I . . . Time flew, Father. I wasn't aware of the lateness of the hour until I saw the clock on the wall and . . . '

'And where, exactly, was this clock on the wall?'

'It was . . . '

Too late, Averil realised her error and her shoulders sagged slightly. Instantly, her inner belief in the validity of her desire for knowledge caused her shoulders to straighten and her chin to jut forward. She was not going to take refuge in lies.

'I was in the library, Father; in the reading room, to be precise. I was reading . . . '

It was foolhardy, she knew, but her inherited spark of the determination that had driven her father to succeed in lifting himself from the ranks of the manual workers to the loftier rank of workshop manager, re-ignited the fire within her.

' . . . about Emily Davison, a brave and wonderful woman who was willing to risk her life to further the cause she believes in.'

There. She'd said it. Her eyes boldly met her father's glare and, although she faltered within, not by one flicker of her eyes did she betray the fact, even when his face darkened with fury.

'Brave and wonderful?' he mocked coldly. 'Foolish and naïve, more like. Risking her own life and that of others in a moment of typical female hysteria. You will not mention her foolish act again within this house, neither in my presence nor out of it. Do you hear me? I said, 'Do you hear me?' '

Averil swallowed but raised her chin a little higher. 'Yes, I hear you, Father.'

His eyes narrowed as he regarded her proud stance and the set expression of her face.

'You will go to your room and stay there for the remainder of the day,' he commanded coldly. 'Furthermore, I forbid you to enter the premises of the public library ever again.'

Averil flinched at that. A temporary confinement to her room was one thing — a permanent exclusion from the public lending library was quite a different matter altogether.

Though her heart was pounding, she met his gaze calmly. 'I'm sorry, Father, but I cannot make a promise to that effect.'

'Cannot? Cannot?' His voice rose high as white-hot anger surged through him. 'I'll teach you, 'cannot'!'

Without warning, his right hand swung hard at her head, catching her ear and cheek in its ferocious blow.

Averil staggered sideways and would have fallen but for the high wooden back of an upright chair that was close to hand. Her head rang with pain and unbidden tears prickled at her eyes. She refused to let them fall and, with an outward show of calm deliberation, she forced herself upright.

'If that is all, Father, I will go to my room.'

Not waiting for permission, she turned on her heel and strode from the room, being careful to let the door shut quietly behind her.

She would have run past the white-faced figure of her mother who was waiting anxiously in the hall if her mother had not put out her hand to touch her.

'Averil?' her mother whispered. 'Oh, Averil! What have you done? He will never forgive you! Never!'

'And I will never forgive him!' Averil spat back, unable any longer to prevent her hot tears falling from her eyes. 'He is hateful! I don't know why you married him!'

Grace sighed. She had had no choice. Her father had arranged her marriage to the up-and-coming young man a little above their station in life. She had had no option but to obey. It was her 'duty', she had been told.

The door of the study was flung open

and Joshua stood framed in the doorway. 'Stand away from your daughter, wife. She is to go to her room and remain within it until I give permission for her to leave it. Is that understood?'

When Grace only nodded mutely, he repeated the question. 'Is that understood?'

Grace nodded again and answered faintly, 'Yes, Joshua.'

'Good. I will have words with you, madam, in here. Immediately.'

Grace released her hold on Averil's arm and somewhat fearfully slipped past her husband into his study.

Averil gathered up the hem of her gown and ran upstairs to the sanctuary of her room. It wasn't the first time he had struck her, but it was the hardest. And, for the time being, her rebellious spirit was quenched as she cried into the feather pillow on her bed.

When the spate of tears had subdued, she rose from her bed and stood by the window, gazing out over Chorley Old Road, the older of the two roads that ran between Horwich and Bolton, and beyond, to where the Pennines came tumbling to an end with Rivington Pike, topped with its small tower, to the left and the softer rolling Rivington moors to the right.

Bathed in sunshine as they were, she longed to be free to stride up George's Lane, past Wallsuches and maybe even to the Pike itself. Certainly to its lower edges which gave such a pleasant view over the Lancashire Plain.

Soon the church clock struck five and, it was with some surprise that she realised it was tea-time. Nothing was brought up to her and she dared not to go down to the kitchen to find something to eat. However, a drink of water was another matter altogether.

She cautiously opened her bedroom door, peeped along the landing to make sure no-one was about, and crept over to the bathroom, which was situated at the rear of the house, between two smaller bedrooms. She knew that not many of the town's houses had plumbed-in bathrooms as they had.

There was also a narrow flight of stairs that led up to two attic rooms. Mary Ellen slept in one of them, unlike Mr and Mrs Hesketh, who rented their own small terraced house in town and came daily to work, counting themselves to be lucky that both of them were in employment.

Averil thought she heard the sound of crying from somewhere but when she strained her ears to listen more attentively, the sound had gone and she decided that she must have imagined it, for who was there to cry except herself?

3

The following day, an outwardly subdued Averil was eventually permitted to leave her room and rejoin her parents downstairs. Rebellion still raged within. She had done nothing very dreadfully wrong.

In a toneless voice, upon her father's insistence, she apologised to him for her behaviour of the previous day. Despite her mother's whispered pleas, she made no promises for the future. Instead, she coolly held her gaze steady, her chin tilted in what her mother feared to be an attitude of defiance that was bound to draw more of her father's wrath upon her.

Joshua made no comment other than to impart notice of further punishment upon his daughter. She was to remain solely within the house until she was willing to promise total obedience to his

will. The manner in which she conducted herself would be the basis of
Joshua's decision as to when to end her
imposed confinement.

To Grace's relief, Averil accepted his
verdict.

Averil had no alternative. She had
noted her mother's bruised and blotched
face but, when her anxious enquiry
brought forth the quiet insistence that
she had walked into the side of a
cupboard, she desisted from further
questioning. She had her own ideas of
the cause of the bruising and realised,
with a sense of shock, that this was not
the first evidence of her father's harsh
treatment of his wife.

She supposed that she had previously
been reluctant to face the matter,
having only acknowledged the verbal
aspect of her father's abuse towards her
mother. Now, coupled with his physical
attack on herself, and the sound of
crying she had heard last night, she
could evade the true conclusion no
longer.

Her father was a brute and a bully.

Her determination not to be subdued by him was strengthened by the memory of James Rushworth's smiling eyes. She shivered with pleasure at the recollection.

By Saturday, Averil's outwardly calm behaviour earned her the right to sit with her mother in the sitting room and, when her friend, Phoebe Mawdsley, came to call, she was allowed to welcome her inside.

Averil could tell that Phoebe was excited about something and, after discussing Emily Davis's heroic act at the Derby, Averil touched Phoebe's arm.

'What have you come to tell me? I can see it is something exciting.'

Phoebe's eyes sparkled. 'You missed a good meeting on Thursday evening. A speaker came from Bolton and told us that there is to be a suffrage rally in Moss Bank Park this afternoon. It is partly to add our voices to Emily Davison's act of protest at the Derby, and to alert the authorities to the fact that we are not to be fobbed off with the Private Member's Bill they have planned for the next parliamentary session in the place of the Reform Bill that they promised and then withdrew. We have been making placards and banners to wave and we are to wear our red, white and green scarves. Do say you can come.'

Averil's face lit up with interest. 'Oh, indeed I must. I have been desperate these past two days. Father confined me to the house, you know, merely because I was late for dinner and had had the temerity to step inside the public library.'

'I knew something had kept you from the meeting. I told Bessie Lord so. Dare you risk coming to Bolton today?'

Averil's imposed solitude of the previous day had done nothing to quench her rebellion against her father's severity, although the thought of his anger if her outing were to be discovered made her face sober slightly. However, if every

36

suffragist balked at the first obstacle, where would their movement be? She need look no further than to Emily Davison.

'I must risk it. It couldn't have happened on a better day. Father is to attend the cricket match at the recreation ground this afternoon. He has been asked to present the shield and be guest of honour at the cricket club tea. So, we are to have dinner promptly at twelve.'

'Good! I knew you would want to come. We're all taking a picnic and you'll need a blanket or rug to sit on.'

Phoebe rose from her seat, her task completed. 'Now, I must go. I've got others to see. Oh, and we're travelling on wagonettes hired from the co-op stables and will be passing here soon after one o'clock. If you're coming, be waiting outside at that time.'

With a delighted smile, Averil ran to the kitchen, quelling any anxious or guilty thoughts. A few anxious moments gripped her whilst her mother considered the matter but, on hearing the names of the NUWSS committee members who were also going, she gave Averil her permission to attend the rally and picnic.

Amazed at her outward calmness, Averil made polite conversation with her father at the dinner table and hoped her mother would not be tempted to inform him of her intended outing.

Nothing was said and, less than half an hour later, as soon as Joshua had departed from the house, Averil collected a packed picnic basket from the kitchen and, with a light rug over her arm, she skipped down the front steps and across the road.

She didn't have long to wait. Three wagonettes, seemingly full of women of all ages and rank and a few valiant men, were pulled up the hill by teams of magnificent shire horses. Averil waved her hand to attract the driver's attention and a madly-waving Phoebe in the second wagonette drew her in that direction.

'I thought you'd missed it,' Phoebe exclaimed, squeezing along the bench to make room for Averil.

'Not likely,' Averil retorted. 'Nothing would keep me away from this.'

Oh, it was wonderful. The ladies alternately chatted and sang their rousing suffrage songs, stopping to pick up other enthusiasts along the route and eventually arrived at their destination, where they spilled out onto the grass and trooped over to the temporary wooden dais that had been erected under the trees.

After a sober start, when prayers were said for Emily Davison and her unfortunate victim, enthusiastic cheers rent the air every time one speaker concluded and another began. Grievances were aired and expounded and plans for future demonstrations made known.

The preparations for a pilgrimage to London, due to take place during the latter half of June and almost the whole of July, were well under way, and an invitation to join the pilgrims was issued anew.

Six weeks on the road was planned. Meetings were to be held at suitable venues on the route and money raised to further the cause.

But Averil knew it was not for her. Her father would disown her. But she could dream about it and cheer them on their way through newspaper reports. It was to culminate in a rally in London's Hyde Park on July twenty-sixth.

'It must be conducted in an orderly manner, ladies. We will not be dragged down by our more militant sisters,' the current speaker implored. 'We must give the authorities no cause to vilify our movement. Seemly conduct and our determination to succeed will win the day.

'And now, ladies, pick up your placards and banners! Twice around the park and then we will picnic on the grass. Enjoy your day.'

Averil, Phoebe and their friends were to the rear of the procession. In high spirits, they flaunted their placards and waved their banners or scarves as they marched along, unmindful of a group of young men who had paused by the animals' corner to watch them.

'Hey-up! Here come t' lasses,' one youth cheered.

The girls lifted their noses slightly higher towards the sky, in prim disdain, though one or two glanced sideways and giggled encouragingly at the youth. They, in turn, now hit upon the occasion to have some sport.

'Have you nowt else to do, lasses? You could come and walk wi' us if you want,' one young fellow called out.

'Aye! Me and my mates could give thee a good time!' another rejoined.

It was all in good humour at first and the girls responded in like manner.

'You could join us later for our picnic,' Emma Ingham rashly promised.

'Eh, we could, at that! Come on, lads!' the young man called, moving forward and encouraging the others to follow.

Emma instantly regretted her invitation. 'No, not yet. Later, after our march around the park.'

'Nay, there's no time like t'present! Let's get it, lads!'

The girls squealed as the young men rushed forward en masse. Too late, they realised that the procession had left them behind whilst they had dallied. They clustered together, getting in each other's way, partly enjoying the confrontation and mock battle, recognising that the young men were only playfully accosting them.

However, it wasn't in their nature to surrender too easily. Playground battles had trained them differently.

Dolly Cocker reached into the basket she carried on her arm and selected a bread bun.

'Have this then,' she laughed as she threw it at the youths.

'And this!' called another, throwing another edible missile.

Before they knew it, a mock battle raged, the procession and their 'seemly behaviour' forgotten. Amidst laughter and shrieks, the two sides pelted each other with cakes and buns. The girls gradually retreated towards the animals' corner, intending to take shelter among the different animal enclosures there.

The sound of breaking glass brought the affray to a sudden end. The girls looked over their shoulders in horror at the shattered pane of glass behind them . . . and then turned accusingly towards the youths.

'You did that. What's the big idea?' Averil challenged them.

'You lot started it!' a youth declared. 'Come on, lads! We're off!'

'Hey! You, there!' came a stern shout. Three park attendants were bearing down upon the girls, their faces red with anger.

The group of girls glanced apprehensively at each other.

'It wasn't us! We didn't do it!' Phoebe hissed. 'Come on! Let's run!'

The girls scattered. Some dropped their baskets, others lost their hats . . . all lost their dignity as they tried to evade capture.

Averil looked over her shoulder as she ran. One of the attendants was pursuing her, clearly not intending to give up his chase lightly.

This was all she needed. She could imagine the headlines in the local newspaper. *Suffragists And Hooligans On The Rampage In Family Park*. All would be named, of course. Her father would take great delight in bemoaning to anyone who cared to listen that his daughter had at last shown herself in her true colours.

She turned left . . . slap bang into the firm body of a young man. It wasn't one of the youths who had sported with them. His clothes were too well cut for that. She raised her head . . . and stepped backwards in confusion. If her face hadn't been already red from exertion, it was now red with embarrassment . . . for the young man was no other than James Rushworth.

James raised his hat. He seemed bemused to see her, especially in the state she was in, though his voice showed concern when he spoke.

'Good afternoon, Miss Townley. Is everything all right? You seem to be, er, a little distraught, shall we say?'

A man's voice shouted from the passageway she had just emerged from. Her head turned in that direction and swiftly back again.

'I'm sorry! I must go! The park attendant . . . he mustn't catch me!'

She tried to push past him but he prevented her.

The touch on her hand was light, but possessive. His dusky eyes seemed to devour her. She wasn't sure how to respond. Her heart pounded and she tried to step back a little.

'Were you part of the fracas I heard back there? The broken glass?'

His eyebrow rose fractionally in amusement, she thought. Really. This was too awful. But it would be worse if the park attendant caught up with her.

'Yes!' she admitted reluctantly. 'Let me go! I must run!'

The pounding of heavy-booted feet

sounded just around the corner. She flung an agonised look in that direction and tried once more to rush on her way.

What happened next quite took her breath away. James enfolded her in his arms, swung their bodies around so that his back was nearest to the would-be captor and pressed his mouth over hers.

Shock was Averil's first emotion! Unalleviated, heart-stopping shock.

Her body stiffened. Had he gone out of his mind? No gentleman would accost a young lady of, well, moderate to upper class, in broad daylight and in such a public place.

His lips were firm and dry, velvety almost, just as she'd known they would be. It was really a very pleasant experience, she began to think, relaxing her body slightly, aware of strange ripples of pleasure coursing around her.

The pounding footsteps paused, Averil felt James' body tense slightly. His lips left hers and his hand pulled her face against his jacket and held it there.

'My good man?' James' voice queried coolly.

'Er, sorry, sir, ma'am. I mean, miss. Sorry!'

Averil squirmed at the embarrassment, censure, even . . . in his voice. Which was worse? To be thought to be a missile-throwing hooligan, or a loose-living woman of low consequence?

Before Averil could make up her mind, James' head once more descended towards hers and the delightful touch of his lips sent more exquisite ripples of joy spiralling through her.

Averil felt the very core of her being to be melting and her legs were surely going to buckle beneath her.

She felt lost. Her senses had left her, and when James gently removed his lips from hers, she felt strangely bereft, stunned even. Did kisses always have that effect?

She stepped away, her face flushing deeply at the thought. How dare he?

The feeling of indignation arising within her overcame the memory of pleasure and she faced him with annoyance. Annoyance that increased as she took in his grinning expression.

'Well, that seemed to do the trick!' he congratulated himself.

'Seemed to do the trick!' Averil echoed. 'You blatantly kiss me in broad daylight and that is all you can say about it.'

James smirked reflectively, his chin cupped between his forefinger and thumb. 'Well, if you press me to say more, I reckon I could think of a few more remarks to say. What would you have me do? Rate your kisses from one to ten?'

His tone was jocular but Averil could only hear derision. Was that what he thought of her?

'There you are, James! Edmund has been waiting for you to play with his ball.'

It was a beautiful, slender, elegantly-clothed young lady, holding the hand of a three or four-year-old boy.

Averil felt her shame to be doubled.

James was married . . . and with a young son. How could he?

Her hand moved without her giving it impetus and the slap was delayed no longer.

4

James watched Averil's fleeing figure, the fingers of his left hand ruefully stroking his reddening cheek.

'Been up to your tricks again, James, dear?' his female companion teased, her right eyebrow arched knowingly.

James laughed. 'Not really.'

'But you'd like to!'

'You know me too well, Lucinda.'

'None better, little brother.'

Lucinda nodded in the direction that Averil had fled. 'Your charms have failed to please this time, I presume?'

'For the moment.' He grinned mischievously, his cheeks dimpling. 'But I'll win in the end. I always do.'

Lucinda sniffed in disapproval. 'It's time you stopped breaking hearts and settled down. Who are you taking to the summer ball at Rivington Hall barn next week?'

James glanced once more in the direction that Averil had fled but her figure was now out of sight.

'Since I didn't know I would be here for the ball, I've not asked anyone yet.' He stroked his chin thoughtfully. 'Maybe I'll go without a partner. You never know who might be there.'

Lucinda laughed lightly. 'Do you know who she is?'

'Oh, yes!'

'So, what game are you playing? You know Papa is desirous of you making a good match.'

James flung her a look of irritation. 'Good heavens, Lucinda, I'm not about to ask the girl to marry me. I hardly know her. She just . . . interests me. She has spirit, a mind of her own, unlike the stream of simpering 'misses' Mamma parades in front of me. She fascinates me.'

'Then, why don't you invite her to the ball, and get her out of your system? She can always say, 'no'.'

It was James' turn to laugh. 'From

the little I know of Miss Townley, she very well might. No, there's a better way.'

Ignoring his sister's quizzical look, he turned to his young nephew. 'Right, Master Edmund. Toss that ball to me and I'll show you how to play football.'

★   ★   ★

The following morning, a somewhat subdued Averil went to church with her parents.

She had managed to arrive home the previous day slightly before her father returned from his social engagement and she knew she had had a narrow escape.

Throughout the night, she alternately blushed with embarrassment and fumed at James' treatment of her. He was a womaniser, a charlatan, a Casanova. She would never forgive him. And as for his poor wife, who was probably made to suffer his roving eye and dalliances with great frequency . . . words failed her!

Determined not to give her father any excuse to renew her punishment of the previous week, she now followed her mother demurely into Joshua's favoured pew and, seated between them, she found the correct page in the service book.

After the service, Averil followed her parents as they made their way along the church path towards the lych gate, pausing momentarily to exchange the usual Sunday greetings between groups of friends, neighbours and acquaintances of her parents' choosing.

A shrill voice arrested their progress and all three turned round to face the one who hailed them. 'Joshua and Grace. So nice to see you. And you, too, Averil. You're looking too pink, dear. Have you been too much in the sun without your hat?'

It was Aunt Clara, the wife of Joshua's younger brother, Henry. Averil wasn't particularly fond of her. She was a social climber who was permanently embittered by her lack of social standing.

Without his older brother's determination to better himself, Henry's position at work remained as a general fitter on the assembly line in the machine shop of the local locomotive works and, to Clara's constant humiliation, went to work dressed in overalls, old jacket and cloth cap.

They had three children. The eldest, Liza was a year younger than Averil. In looks, both girls took after their paternal grandmother. Like Averil, Liza had abundant chestnut curls that fell as ringlets from under her bonnet, but the prettiness of her features was too often marred by a petulant expression and her character was much too like her mother's to make her counted amongst Averil's close friends. Harry, aged ten, and Jessie, aged eight, were likeable children.

Arm in arm with one of her friends, heads close as they giggled together, Liza joined the family group. She singled out Averil and drew her slightly apart from their elders.

'Does Uncle Joshua know you were at the suffragist rally yesterday?' she asked, her eyes sliding sideways to see if her question had been overheard by any of the adults.

'No, he doesn't! And don't you dare tell him, Liza! I'll never forgive you, if you do.' Averil hissed back. 'Anyway, how do you know? I didn't see you there.'

'I should think not.' Liza retorted. 'You won't catch me at such events.'

'Don't try to be so superior, Liza. You don't know what you're talking about. We are fighting for women's rights. Doesn't it bother you that you will always be under your father's authority until you are married? And then under your husband's until the day you die?'

'Why should it? I get my own way pretty well as it is, and I'll make sure I marry someone who has loads of money, so I shan't care what he says. Besides, I've heard that most husbands like to have the occasional dalliance, and so shall I.'

Averil was shocked. She pressed her lips together, remembering with shame that she had been an unintentional part of such a thing only the previous day.

'Well, I shall only marry for love,' she stated firmly.

Liza laughed at her outraged expression. 'You're such a prude, Averil. You'll never get a man with your missish ways!' She caught sight of a darkly-clad figure who was approaching them with a hopeful smile on his face. 'At least, not a man worthy of the name!'

She nudged Averil with her elbow, grinning broadly. 'Here comes your loyal admirer. Maybe you should put him out of his misery and accept his 'approaches' before he goes into a decline.'

Averil followed the direction of Liza's gaze and groaned within. Oliver Markham. He was nearly forty, she was sure. He had lived with his mother until her death last year and now he was seeking a replacement 'housekeeper'. Or so the local gossip went. Why he thought he stood a chance with her, she had no idea.

She hastily hailed Phoebe, who had just emerged from the church, but Phoebe took one look at who was about to claim Averil's attention and spread out her hands in a regretful action.

'Judas!' Averil mouthed at her, and at Liza's back, as her cousin joined another group of young women.

'Ah, Miss Townley.' Mr Markham greeted her. 'How delightful to meet you on this glorious summer's day. You are an embodiment of all of nature's joy, my dear. May I show my appreciation?'

Without pause he grabbed hold of her hand and drew it towards his lips.

Averil could barely resist shuddering, remembering the flabby, moist lips that had touched her skin on a previous occasion when she had been completely unprepared.

'Really, Mr Markham! You mustn't

be so forward with me,' she reproved him sharply.

She unconsciously wiped her hand on the fabric of her skirt, striving to suppress the grimace of distaste that she knew was upon her face. The incident unnerved her and her eyes frantically searched the nearby groups of parishioners for a needy distraction but none responded.

She noted that Liza was now among a group of giggling young ladies who were casting repeated glances her way and her face flushed with a mixture of anger and embarrassment. She drew back her shoulders and lifted her chin.

'Excuse me, Mr Markham. I must rejoin my family.'

She knew she sounded haughty but it was her only defence. She nodded curtly and made to move away.

'Oliver, please. Call me Oliver, Miss Townley.' He loped sideways, his body bobbing up and down as he kept pace with her movements. 'Your sensibility is to be admired, Miss Townley. Yes, indeed. To be much admired. I must speak to your father. Yes, that is the way. Excuse me, Miss Townley. Excuse me.'

Averil abruptly halted, almost causing Mr Markham to stumble. 'Speak to my father? What on earth for?'

'Why, to discuss, to discuss, business matters,' he stammered.

Averil relaxed. Well, that was all right. 'He won't want to speak with you on a Sunday, though,' she felt compelled to advise him.

Mr Markham hesitated, his face displaying a glimmer of hope. 'When would you suggest I approach him, Miss Townley? Tomorrow?'

'I really couldn't say. I suggest you make an appointment with him.'

She smiled tightly, not wishing to give him any encouragement to persist with his amorous intentions towards her. With any luck, she would know when he was coming and could arrange to be out. Remembering her manners, she nodded her head slightly.

'Goodbye, Mr Markham.'

She knew she should have given him her hand in a farewell gesture but forbore to do so. Instead, she tossed her head high and strolled with forced gaiety over to where her mother was extricating herself from Clara's over-solicitous enquiries about the fading bruise on her chin.

Monday's newspaper announced the shocking news that Emily Davison had died of her injuries. Averil felt devastated. She hurried round to visit Phoebe, and together they made their way to the house of the NUWSS chairwoman, Mrs Leatherbarrow.

Averil soon had another matter to take her attention for, on Tuesday, Joshua received a hand-delivered, gold-edged card inviting him and his wife and daughter to the summer ball at Rivington Hall barn to be held the coming Saturday evening.

'Why us?' Grace mused quietly. 'We have never been invited before.'

Joshua cast her a disparaging look. 'It is obviously in recognition of my social and charitable works. And, long overdue it is. But, no matter. It has come at last.'

He glanced critically at his wife. 'I sincerely hope you will acquit yourself favourably, and you must instruct Averil on the correct social etiquette. I won't be having either of you letting down our family name.'

Grace inwardly fumed at her husband's low opinion of her and Averil, but was careful not to let it show in her facial expression.

'Of course, dear. Averil knows perfectly well how to behave beautifully.'

'When she chooses.' He frowned and read the invitation again. 'Maybe we should go without her. I haven't forgotten her disgraceful behaviour of last week.'

Grace knew better than to argue with her husband. She affected an air of compliance. 'As you wish, dear. What shall I write in our response letter? That Averil is unwell? A pity. There will be some well-to-do families there. You never know.'

'Hmm. I wonder if Oliver Markham will be there?' he murmured thoughtfully.

'Oliver Markham? What has he to do with it?' Joshua tapped the card against his hand. 'I think it may be due to him that this invitation has come our way.' He coughed gruffly. 'You may tell Averil that she is to attend the ball, but say nothing else. It is best left as a simple invitation.'

He waved his hand dismissively. 'Be gone, woman. I'm sure you'll find much to do in preparation, but not too much expense, d'you hear!'

Averil was amazed and delighted to hear of the invitation. 'The summer ball? At Rivington Hall barn?'

'Yes, dear. Isn't it wonderful?'

'It is!' Her initial surprise was suddenly clouded by suspicion. 'I wonder how Father has managed it? What is he up to?'

'He was as surprised as you are, dear. Though I think he may have his suspicions. Time will only tell. However . . . '

She smiled brightly. 'Let's take a look in our wardrobes and see what we can find.'

Fortunately, Grace was nimble with a needle, and by Friday evening two perfectly respectable gowns were hanging on the wardrobe doors. Grace's was of dark red satin, admirably fitting her slender form. Matching elbow-length gloves were folded over the hanger in readiness.

Averil's gown was of pale blue silk-satin. Its high-waist was emphasised by a cream silk cummerbund that had started life as one of Grace's scarves. Averil swung around in front of the mirror, watching the gathered skirt of the embroidered muslin overdress swirl out around her.

'Oh, Mamma, it's beautiful. You're so clever. Thank you!'

With a suspicion of tears in her eyes, she impulsively flung her arms around her mother and hugged her.

Grace responded briefly before gently disentangling herself. Joshua frowned upon an overplay of affection and Grace was unused to experiencing such.

'Get away with you, child. Its beauty has little to do with me. Now, are the sleeves the right length? And the gloves?'

Averil laughed in delight. 'Perfectly, Mamma. It's all perfect. Why, I feel like . . . like a princess.'

'Then watch out for Prince Charming.' Grace warned playfully, enjoying her daughter's enjoyment.

Saturday seemed to take a long time coming. And the day itself dragged slowly . . . until five o'clock, that was. After that, time speeded up and there seemed not time to wash and dress and have a little powder and cream applied.

Grace dressed Averil's hair in curls piled up on her head and held in place by a cream-coloured velvet ribbon with its ends dangling at the back.

Joshua, with uncharacteristic largesse, hired a motorised cab to transport them to Rivington Hall.

Averil enjoyed the ride tremendously.

She couldn't help comparing the vehicle with the more stylish sports car that James Rushworth was driving when she first met him and wondered if she had been too prudish in refusing his offer to take her home.

5

When Lord Lever, a local benefactor, created a park for the inhabitants of Horwich and Bolton to freely enjoy, he opened up to them a world hitherto unknown. He imported wild and exotic animals . . . zebras, lions, gazelles, deer, buffaloes, emus, yaks and many others and set them in enclosures within the park.

Also within the park were two Saxon tithe barns. Rivington Hall barn and the slightly smaller barn, situated lower down on the road that ran to Rivington village, had been converted into refreshment rooms for the convenience of the many visitors who came to enjoy the rural beauty of the Lever Park.

And to think that of all this came from a man whose family had made their fortune by manufacturing soap, Averil mused in wonder.

Following other guests, the Townleys found themselves in the splendid interior of the Hall barn. Hanging baskets of flowers hung from the huge rafter beams that were held in place by massive wooden supports that rose from the floor right up to the roof, high above their heads, and garlands of flowers, coiled around the supporting beams, scented the air with their fragrance.

Joshua strutted as uprightly as his arthritic bones would allow, nodding condescendingly to men of his acquaintance whom he passed as he made his way through the tables.

Averil followed, all the while gazing around at the other guests. The gentlemen were dressed almost as one in their black suits, frilled white shirts and black bow ties.

Her gaze passed on to the ladies, whose gowns were of every colour and shade imaginable, with a great deal more flesh showing than she had ever seen before, making her neckline seem almost modest in comparison.

The tables were arranged around the outer edge of the room, leaving the centre of the room free for dancing, and Joshua strode to what Averil was sure was far too prominent a place and seated himself with great aplomb.

The room was filling nicely and the small orchestra began to play. One or two couples stepped on to the dance floor and began to swirl around it.

The heady atmosphere intoxicated Averil's senses. As her eyes swung further around the room, she saw that the smooth wooden dance-floor continued out through two sets of open french windows into the garden beyond. More small tables were set and Chinese lanterns hung from the trees. People, mainly young ones, were dancing out there.

'Oh, look.' She exclaimed. 'Can't we sit outside, Father? It would be so . . . ' Romantic was the word that hovered on her lips but she knew better than to speak it.

Joshua's glance quelled the question and Averil sank back on to her seat.

The floor was filling up and a slight stir among people seated nearer the entrance heralded the entrance of Lord and Lady Lever, who graciously took to the floor and twirled around it.

Before Averil had had time to imagine herself to be the pitiful lonely sight she dreaded, the first of a steady stream of young men begged her hand for a dance. She was relieved to find that, although they were more accomplished than she was, they didn't seem unduly put out by her hesitant style.

As she circled the floor she let her eyes search among the clusters of dancers and onlookers for the one young man who would make her heart beat erratically, but without success.

James Rushworth was not there.

Just after the supper dance had been announced, she realised that her father was rising to his feet smiling genially and she turned around to determine the cause. To her intense dismay, Oliver

Markham was confidently approaching their table, a beaming smile upon his florid face. She turned to her father, sensing that the meeting had been planned beforehand.

'Father?'

'You are honoured, Averil.'

'But, Father . . . '

'I insist you behave with propriety, Averil.' He hissed in her ear. 'This could lead to a propitious arrangement.'

'What sort of . . . ?'

Joshua was already moving forward, his hand outstretched. 'Mr Markham. How do you do, my good fellow? And how delightful to see you here.'

'How d'you do, Mr Townley? Mrs Townley, ma'am?' He bowed briefly over their heads and turned to Averil. 'And Miss Townley. How ravishingly beautiful you are, my dear. Will you do me the honour of bestowing your good person into my hands for the duration of this dance?'

Averil felt as though all of her blood

had drained from her head. With a sinking heart, she knew that her evening was ruined. Trying very hard to smile pleasantly, she arose from her seat and gave her right hand to Oliver Markham. His touch was warm and clammy as he drew her on to the dance floor, bringing a tiny flicker of distaste to Averil's face.

'I'm afraid I'm not an accomplished dancer,' she murmured quietly.

'You're being coy, Miss Townley.' Oliver reproved her with a smile. 'I have been watching you. I'm sure you will be as light as thistledown in my arms.'

The dance was a waltz, the steps of which Averil knew better than any other, but it always seemed to her the most intimate of ballroom dances, and any show of intimacy was the last thing she wanted to encourage with her present partner. Her fears were well-founded. Oliver grasped her waist with his right hand, holding her far closer than Averil thought proper, and began to propel her backwards.

Averil wondered why she had both-
ered to apologise about her lack of skill.
Although the music was quite lively,
Oliver ploughed his way down to the
outer edge of the dance floor with a
pace and rhythm all of his own. At the
first corner, he clumsily steered her into
a quarter circle and then recommenced
his former style.

Averil wished the floor would open
up and swallow her and tried not to
wince every time he stood on her toes.

It was during a pedantic turn at one
of the corners that Averil felt her gaze
drawn towards a couple approaching
the dance floor. The man, a stranger to
her, had his arm possessively around
the young woman's waist and, if the
loving expression on the woman's face
was anything to go by, she was pleased
to have it so.

With a start, Averil realised that the
young woman was the same as the one
who had been with James in the park at
Bolton. She could see a band of gold
encircling the woman's third finger of

her left hand where it rested lightly on her partner's shoulder. Averil's heart leaped with a sense of joy, even before her mind had decided that, unless the woman was flagrantly flouting all rules of society, this man was her husband, not James!

The realisation sent a rush of effervescent bubbles dancing through Averil's veins, dispelling her earlier pessimism.

In that same instant she knew he was here.

Almost immediately, her eyes were drawn to one of the french windows that led outside, not more than two yards away. Her heart skipped a beat. James Rushworth was leaning nonchalantly against the pillar, his eyes dancing with laughter — insufferable man.

She cheekily let the tip of her tongue peep through her lips in his direction. James laughed more openly and straightened his posture.

As Averil was solidly propelled farther away from him, she saw James straighten the lapels of his jacket and stride after them, murmuring excuses as he manoeuvred past the other dancers. His face bore a look of amused determination and Averil found herself unable to tear her gaze away from him. What was he going to do?

She didn't have to wait long. As he caught up with them, James tapped Oliver on his shoulder.

'Excuse me.'

Oliver jumped and stepped once more on to Averil's toes.

'P . . . pardon?'

'It's a 'gentleman's excuse me' dance.' James replied with a curt nod. 'May I have the pleasure, Miss Townley?'

Averil felt a hysterical giggle rising up in her throat. It wasn't an 'excuse me'. But it was too good an offer to turn down.

'Certainly, sir,' she dimpled mischievously.

As soon as James took her in his arms, Averil knew he would be a good dancer. His hold was firm and intimate.

A tiny gasp escaped her lips as James' right hand drew her waist towards him and moulded her body into his. Strange, delightful sensations fizzed and sparkled within her. Did he feel it, too?

Her startled gaze flew to his face. He was grinning mischievously at her.

'Just relax against me and let me lead you,' he whispered in her ear.

His warm breath tickled her skin. She remembered the velvet touch of his lips on hers and moved imperceptively nearer to him, letting a sigh of pleasure dip through her lips.

It was matched by a small murmur of satisfaction from James.

They were weaving through the other dancers, though Averil was scarcely aware of them. She felt as though she were floating, though she knew that was impossible.

Averil was aware of nothing but themselves. Her eyes were fixed on his. They were like deep, dark pools of danger and delight.

'Have I told you that you're the

prettiest girl here?' James whispered. 'I'm the envy of every man present.'

'Are you?' she breathed, feeling it was her who was the envy of every young woman under the age of twenty-five, and probably of many who were appreciably older.

So mesmerised was she by the wondrous sensations and the heady intimacy of their physical closeness, that she completely forgot that she had begun to dance with another man and, if her parents had seen her whirl by in the arms of someone they hadn't met, they would be wondering what had happened to Oliver.

The dance music was slowing down and Averil knew a sense of disappointment. She felt unprepared to be separated from James so soon. A sense of panic spread through her.

Although she spoke no word, James seemed to sense her thoughts. They were approaching the open french windows and, as the orchestra swung into the second tune, James steered

Averil through the opening into the freshness of the evening air.

As Averil relaxed, his gaze locked on her face. It was ablaze with excitement and James felt a thrill of invincibility surge through him, tempered by a glow of . . . he almost thought 'love', but that held the bondage of commitment, so he banished the word and replaced it with 'passion'.

Averil's left hand remained resting lightly upon his shoulder and James' right hand remained around her waist but their other hands reluctantly dropped, although James still held her close.

'Are you hungry?' he asked, raising his right eyebrow quizzically. His left hand rose and he gently drew his finger down the right side of her face and along her jaw line, letting it pause under her chin. He tilted her face up to his, smiling into her eyes.

'Not especially so,' Averil breathed softly.

'Then let's walk in the garden,' he suggested, drawing her in that direction. 'We can grab a bite of supper when everyone else has had theirs.'

The heavy perfume of roses filled the warm air. The evening sky was darkening slightly, though it was still light enough to see.

Suddenly, James wanted to know everything about her. What made her smile? What made her happy, or sad? What were her thoughts on current affairs?

'Tell me about yourself,' he invited. 'All I know is your name.'

'There's not much more to know,' Averil laughed. 'I'm nineteen. I've no brothers or sisters. My father is very strict with me and Mamma is gentle and kind but very much under Father's thumb.'

They paused from walking and stood smiling at each other in mutual satisfaction. They had left the rose garden and were now among some taller trees that edged a small clearing. A summerhouse stood only a few yards away.

Averil wondered if James intended to invite her inside it, but the sound of light laughter betrayed the presence of other lovers.

As if reading her thoughts, James leaned back against a tree and drew her to him. Averil's heart raced. She hoped he was going to kiss her again. This time she wouldn't spoil it by slapping his face.

'You're a beautiful young lady,' James said huskily. 'I took advantage of your situation last Saturday, but I meant no disrespect. I wanted to kiss you the first time we met.'

'Did you?' Averil breathed, lifting her face.

James lowered his head to her and gently covered her mouth with his. It was all Averil remembered, and more. Wild sensations ran through her body. Icy tingles met with molten fire and her mind fizzed and sparkled.

Averil felt on fire. It was the most wonderful sensation she had ever experienced but she suddenly felt alarmed. Everything was moving too fast, out of her control. She wasn't sure what it all meant and panicked suddenly.

James felt her alarm and lifted his

head. 'It's all right,' he whispered. 'I won't do anything to harm you.'

An enraged roar from behind her drowned Averil's gasp of surprise. 'Averil Townley! How dare you disport yourself in this disgraceful manner?'

Even before she had turned around, Averil recognised her father's voice. The look of fury on his face made her tremble and her body swayed and James' hand saved her from falling.

'Step aside from my daughter, sir! I'll have words with you later.'

'I meant no harm, Mr Townley. We were . . . '

'I saw what you were doing. Your morals belong in the gutter, sir. Release my daughter and be gone.'

James felt Averil try to tug her hand free but was reluctant to let her go, convinced that her father's anger would drive him to harm her.

'Averil was in no way to blame, Mr Townley. I take full responsibility for what happened, and I assure you . . . '

'Assure me? Assure me?' Joshua

challenged James, derision in his voice. 'Of what do you assure me? Do you intend to marry my daughter? Is that what you wish to assure me?'

Averil gasped in mortification. 'Father! Please!'

James hesitated in confusion. 'I . . . ' His grip on Averil's hand loosened, his body rigid with shock.

Averil's hands flew to cover her burning face, her fingers spread across her mouth and cheeks.

'It's clear that you don't.' Joshua thundered. 'So do you mind removing yourself from this situation and leaving my daughter to the care of her fiancé?'

James stared at Averil's horrified face. 'Fiancé?' he queried.

'No!' Averil gasped. 'No! It's not . . . '

'Come, Averil. I will take care of you,' another voice spoke.

Stepping forward from behind Joshua was the portly figure of Oliver Markham and, behind him, was the stricken figure of her mother.

6

Grace hurried forward and put her arm around Averil's shoulder. 'Come back inside, dear. It's getting chilly out here.'

She nervously drew her away from her husband's angry presence, drawing her in the general direction of the Hall barn.

Averil turned, looking for James, but he had gone from the scene. With a strangled sob that hurt her throat, her body drained of all resistance, and she allowed her mother to lead her into the Hall barn through a side door.

Their coats were collected from the cloakroom, a cab was called, and the family returned to their home in silence. Once inside their house, Averil hurried towards the stairs, only to be halted by Joshua's cold voice.

'Inside my study, miss.'

Averil longed for the courage to

disobey but, deep inside, she felt to be in turmoil, one emotion running into another.

'Joshua, won't tomorrow do?' Grace tried to delay the interview.

'I'll have no interference from you, woman,' Joshua barked at her. 'You've done enough harm with your soft treatment of her.'

He flung open the door to his study and stood holding it ajar.

Averil felt a surge of her spirit strengthen her. She tilted her head high and swept into the room with as much assurance as she could muster. She wasn't beaten yet. Even so, the last thing she wanted was a heated argument with her father.

She was careful to stand on the far side of her father's desk, instinctively using it as a barrier between them. Biting nervously on her lower lip, she faced him bravely, with more than a little defiance.

'Well?' Joshua demanded. 'What have you to say for yourself, miss? Behaving like a strumpet. A fine show you made of us.'

'It wasn't I who made the show, Father,' she said quietly, forcing her throat to work, though it hurt her tightened muscles.

Joshua slammed his fist on to the desktop. 'Don't contradict me, girl! You behaved no better than a woman of low repute, bringing scandal to our name. I'll have no more of it, do you hear. Oliver Markham will put paid to that.'

A cold chill struck Averil's heart, jolting her mind. 'Oliver Markham? What concern is it of his? He is nothing to me.'

'Nothing? Nothing? He's the means of scraping your honour out of the gutter, my girl! Showing great forbearance and magnanimity, he has vowed to stand by his earlier offer for your hand.'

'Earlier offer?' Averil's voice was no more than a squeak. She stared unbelievingly at her father, her face drained white.

'Be thankful he has so generous a

character. No-one else would offer for you after tonight's show!' He placed both hands on the edge of his desk and leaned across it. 'I have accepted his proposal on your behalf.'

Averil involuntarily took a step backwards, her hands held in front of her as if warding off a physical attack.

'No! No! Never!'

She pulled herself together and made a movement to push past her father to escape from his presence and this appalling statement, but Joshua blocked her way and she stepped back again.

'I will not marry Mr Markham. I don't even like him, let alone love him.'

Joshua snorted disparagingly. 'Love? Don't talk to me of love. It's obedience I insist on from you, my girl. Obedience. And I shall have it. Mr Markham will accompany us home after church tomorrow and he will speak to you in private, and you will accept his proposal with due thankfulness for his generous disposition in being willing to overlook your loose behaviour tonight.'

Averil listened in growing distaste, horror, even. He couldn't mean it! It wasn't possible!

'No!' she repeated. 'I can't. I won't. You can't make me!'

'I can, and I will! You will do as I tell you, or else!'

Averil faced him, her expression cold. 'Or else what, Father? You will hit me again? As you hit Mamma?'

Joshua's face reddened in anger. His clenched fist hit the desktop once more. 'It is my right as your father to chastise you and punish your wilful behaviour. I'll not shirk my duty, and you will obey. Otherwise, I shall disown you. I'll cut you off without a penny.'

The idea was so preposterous that Averil scarcely took it in. It was all too much. The evening's events had drained her and she knew that to argue further would lead her nowhere. Her father was too dogmatic to reason with and he would not climb down. She drew herself up tall.

'Is that all, Father? May I retire to my room now?'

Her quiet response seemed to flummox him and he replied coolly. 'Aye, get to your room.'

Averil left the room without looking at her father and without speaking. Grace was anxiously hovering in the hall. Averil made as if to speak to her but her father's voice bellowed, 'I'll see you in here, madam, at once.'

Grace cast an anxious glance at Averil's drawn features and then hurried into the study.

Averil stared blankly at the closed door, unable to fully comprehend what had happened. Then, with a sob, she gathered up the hem of her skirt and ran upstairs.

By morning, Averil had determined what to do. Further argument with her father would avail nothing. She dressed carefully and, with composed features, went downstairs to breakfast.

She wasn't aware of any part of the morning service at church, though she stood or kneeled at the proper times and held her open hymn book and prayer book in her hand.

Phoebe tried to attract her attention without success and wondered what had happened to her friend to cause such white-faced withdrawal.

At the end of the service, Oliver Markham appeared at her side and invited her to walk up the hill with him. Under her father's glaring eyes, she quietly agreed, though she refused the offer of his arm and spoke only in quiet expressionless monosyllables in response to Oliver's fatuous conversation.

Joshua invited Oliver into the living room with false joviality and Grace made nervous conversation, casting apprehensive glances at Averil, who sat primly on the edge of her seat, taking no part in the stilted conversation.

At last, Joshua rose from his chair. 'Come, Grace. We have dinner to see to.'

Averil nearly laughed. Her father did nothing towards preparing dinner, not ever, but her mother obediently followed him from the room.

Silence prevailed.

The clock on the mantelpiece loudly ticked the time away.

Mr Markham coughed discreetly. 'I'm sure your father has prepared you for what I am about to say,' he began.

Averil looked straight ahead.

'And he has, er, led me to believe that my address will not be unwelcome.'

Averil casually glanced at him. 'Really?'

Encouraged by this, Mr Markham hastily dropped on one knee in front of Averil and took hold of her right hand where it lay cool and still on her lap.

'Miss Townley, Averil, my dear. I am willing to overlook your unladylike behaviour of last evening and am willing to concede that it was an indication of your naîvety of worldly matters and not a deliberate act of loose morality. No doubt you were overwhelmed by the attentions of . . . that young man . . . who, I might add, behaved deplorably towards you and deserves to be horsewhipped and . . . '

'Oh, do get on with it, Mr Markham,' Averil said impatiently.

'Pardon? Oh, yes, yes, of course, only do call me Oliver, since we are about to be betrothed.'

Averil sighed and made a move as if to stand up.

'Miss Townley, will you do me the honour of becoming my wife? I think we must be married as soon as possible to divert attention away . . . '

'No, Mr Markham,' Averil said quietly but firmly and then continued briskly. 'Now, if that was all, may I suggest that we stop this ridiculous charade and go into dinner?'

'N . . . no? W . . . what do you mean, no?'

'Exactly that, Mr Markham. I refuse your offer.'

She searched her mind for some polite but unequivocal words. 'I am conscious of the, er, honour you offer me, but the answer is, no, I will not become your wife!'

'B . . . but . . . your father . . . '

'Was obviously mistaken.'

Averil stood up, causing Mr Markham to hastily shuffle backwards and stagger to his feet.

'But, Miss Townley, maybe you didn't fully understand. Your father . . . '

'Mr Markham, my father has allowed you to suffer a misapprehension. I do not love you. Indeed, I hardly know you, and you do not know me.' She laughed shortly. 'Maybe if you did know me, you would realise how mismatched we would be.'

'But, Mr Townley . . . '

' . . . gave you false expectations. I am sorry but I have nothing else to say.'

Mr Markham's expression tightened and closed. 'Then I must bid you good-day.'

He backed away from her towards the door. Averil almost felt sorry for him but knew it would be futile to say so.

Mr Markham straightened his jacket

and tie. 'Pray give my apologies to your good parents. I find I cannot, cannot stay to dinner after all.'

Averil held herself rigid, unable to relax her stance. She heard the front door open and close and waited for what seemed to be an age before the living room door opened and her father stepped hesitantly into the room.

'What has happened? Where is Mr Markham?'

'He has gone, Father.'

'Gone? What do you mean? Gone where?'

'To his home, I expect. He didn't exactly say where he was going.'

'Why has he gone?' Joshua's voice rose with each word. 'What did you say to him?'

'I refused his offer of marriage,' Averil said coolly. 'He made his proposal, which, I might say, bordered on insolent condescension. I declined, and he went.'

Joshua's face reddened. The veins in his neck and head bulged alarmingly.

'Insolent condescension? After your behaviour last night? How dare you?' he shouted. He stepped forward, raising his fist as if to strike her.

Averil jerked away but the movement was unnecessary.

Joshua's eyes seemed to stare unseeingly and he staggered sideways, grasping for the wing of the nearest chair, but he missed and crashed to the floor.

It was mid-afternoon before Averil and Grace were able to sink into two easy chairs and thankfully drink the cups of tea that Mrs Hesketh had brewed for them.

The doctor had been, declared that Joshua had suffered a stroke, and then helped them to dismantle a single bed, carry it downstairs and reassemble it in Joshua's study.

'I suggest you make this room into a temporary bedchamber, Mrs Townley,' the doctor advised. 'Your husband will need careful nursing, and I must warn you that his age stands against him.'

'Oh!' Grace gave a little cry and held

out a hand towards Averil.

At long last, when Joshua was settled in his bed and Mrs Hesketh took a turn at sitting with him, Grace and Averil managed to spend a few minutes together.

'I warned you not to cross him, Averil,' Grace remonstrated quietly. 'And now look what has happened!'

'How can you support him in this, Mamma,' Averil protested. 'Would you, too, have me marry a pompous man whom I cannot love?'

'Would it be all that too hard to bear? I have lived these thirty years with Joshua. I haven't fared too badly, and there is a greater difference in our ages.'

'Mamma! He is a tyrant! He has made your life a misery!'

'If I had given him a son, he would have treated me better.'

'It takes two to make a baby. You are no more to blame than he.'

Grace patted her hand and smiled faintly. 'I'm sure Mr Markham wouldn't treat you so, Averil. He professes to be quite fond of you.'

'But he doesn't know me, Mamma! He would stifle me. There is so much more for women to do these days, and more to come. We really will have the right to vote one day, and be able to use our brains in matters more important than reckoning up our butcher's bill.'

★　★　★

Over the next two days, Joshua made little progress, and Averil was surprised to learn that he had made signs to make himself understood that he wished to summon his solicitor.

'He wants to be sure his affairs are in order,' her mother explained.

The man came and spent over an hour with Joshua. When his work was concluded, he left as quietly as he came.

During the night, there was a severe deterioration in Joshua's condition and on Wednesday morning, a tearful Grace told Averil that he had passed away in the night.

'I am sorry, Mamma,' Averil confronted her. 'I know I was far from being a dutiful daughter to him and cannot pretend to have loved him, but I know you will miss him.'

'I just don't know what to do!' Grace cried. 'He never allowed me to have any say in running our home, or anything. I don't know where to start.'

'I'm sure Uncle Henry will help you, Mamma.'

Uncle Henry, Aunt Clara and Liza visited later that evening. After solemnly viewing the body, they trooped into the living-room and sat stiffly upon three chairs. Aunt Clara fixed a stern gaze on Averil.

'Your face betrays little show of sorrow, Averil,' she reprimanded.

'My sorrow is for Mamma, Aunt Clara,' Averil quietly responded. 'And I will do my best to support her.'

'Hmm.' Clara sniffed. She turned her attention to Grace, casting her eyes around the high-ceilinged room. 'Well, I hope Joshua has left you well-provided for, Grace. I'm sure this house takes a fortune to run. Maybe you'll sell? It's far too large a house for two.'

Grace looked too upset to respond and Averil spoke for her. 'It's too early to think of changes, Aunt.'

'Well, don't expect any help from us. Henry has few enough hours for relaxation as it is, since he is still a working man.'

'Eh, now, Clara, don't be so hard on t'lass. 'Course I'll help thee, our Averil. You've only to ask.' Uncle Henry offered.

'Thank you, Uncle Henry. The funeral is on Monday,' Averil informed them. 'The Co-Operative funeral directors are taking care of everything. And the wake will be held here. You are invited to the reading of the will immediately afterwards, of course.'

'Well, I hope he has thought of us in death, he did little enough for his brother in life,' Clara snapped irritably.

During the course of the following day, cards and letters of condolence began to arrive, one of which was from Oliver Markham.

'There, he is thinking of us,' Grace proclaimed. 'He is going to call.'

'Then be so good as to inform him that I am indisposed.'

*   *   *

James Rushworth had struggled against himself unsuccessfully since Saturday evening. Pride and self-preservation had told him to forget Averil Townley. His heart told him otherwise. Although he had known her for so short a time, he found that life without the hope of seeing her was dull indeed.

He was sure she hadn't lied to him. She wasn't engaged to be married. She couldn't be. She was too full of fun and trustingly naïve to have tried to beguile him.

His mind made up to visit her, he felt wonderfully released from the heaviness that had suffocated him. He drove with a light heart towards Horwich. He would get down on his knees and grovel if he had to.

He wasn't totally sure which house was the Townleys' but the sight of a portly figure entering through the wrought-iron gate of a house just ahead, told him all he needed to know. It was Averil's suitor, Oliver Markham. Undeterred, he drew into the kerb and switched off the engine.

Oliver scowled at him. 'You have a nerve, coming here, young man. I hold you totally responsible for leading Miss Townley astray in that disgraceful manner.'

James coolly regarded him, one eyebrow rising sardonically. He had the satisfaction of seeing Oliver look discomfited.

'I have come to speak to Mr Townley. Any apologies for my part in the unfortunate incident will be addressed to him. Now, if you don't mind . . .'

James made it clear that he was to be

allowed access to the front door.

Oliver, however, stood his ground, forcibly blocking his access. 'You have come too late. Mr Townley passed away yesterday.'

James was taken aback but he stood his ground. 'Then I must offer my condolences to Mrs and Miss Townley,' he said.

Oliver's eyes narrowed slightly and he allowed a small smile to flutter over his lips as he made a swift calculated chance that James was ignorant of the temporary rift between himself and Averil Townley.

'I am sure you will understand that Mrs and Miss Townley have no wish to see anyone other than family at this trying time. I will pass on your condolences, if you wish,' he added magnanimously, 'though I'm not sure that they will be agreeably received, since you are, in part, responsible for Mr Townley's untimely death.'

Although he was shocked by this announcement, James drew himself fully upright, towering over Oliver Markham. 'I would, nevertheless, like to speak to Miss Townley myself,' he said firmly.

Oliver refused to move. 'I'm afraid I cannot allow it,' He smirked openly. 'I am now responsible for Miss Townley's well-being. She will be guided by my decisions, and I refuse to allow you access to her. Is that understood?'

James' spirit sank. He was too late. Oliver Markham had the upper hand. As Averil's fiancé, he was now in command. James turned abruptly away and strode over to his motorcar. He had lost her.

7

Oliver's smug satisfaction was short-lived. In spite of Grace's entreaties on his behalf, Averil refused to leave her room to speak with him.

Oliver was furious. Highly indignant at the treatment meted out to him, he left the house, vowing never to return.

The next few days passed in a blur. Grace wept copiously and Averil found herself remembering moments of happiness with her father in her younger days, even missing his presence around the house, and although she couldn't pretend to be inconsolable at his death, she wept with her mother and shared her grief.

It was somewhat of a relief when the day of the funeral arrived. For all Joshua's home life had been strict and almost loveless, his standing in the community was high and many former colleagues from work and some of the town's dignitaries were there in attendance to express their condolences to his family.

After the funeral, Mr Middleton, their family solicitor, murmured that it was time for the reading of the will and would they take their seats that had been set out in the study.

Henry led Grace to her seat at the front, before sitting behind her with Clara, Liza, Harry and Jessie. Mr Middleton moved slowly through the opening pleasantries and minor bequests. His monotonous tone droned in the warm room and Averil's mind began to wander.

She had hoped that James might have attended the funeral, even though no written word had been received from him. Surely he must have heard of her father's death. It had been on the front page of the local newspaper. She sighed, accepting forlornly that he had been successfully warned off by her father's harshness at the ball.

Mr Middleton cleared his throat,

dragging Averil's attention back to the reading of the will. She thought the solicitor looked uncomfortable and felt the first stirring of misgivings but she hastily dismissed them as nonsensical.

'And now to the, er, house and contents.'

Mr Middleton paused again and looked down at the document he was holding in front of him. 'The house, known as 'Collinswood', and all its contents are left to my brother, Henry Townley, with the proviso that he provides a home for my wife, Grace Townley, for the duration of her lifetime, with a private allowance to be reviewed annually.'

An audible gasp sounded from all adults.

Averil felt that surely she must have misheard, but, in that case, so had everyone else. Her mother had gone white. She jerked her glance to the row behind and could see that Henry was equally stunned.

Liza was grinning with excitement.

'Does that mean this house is ours now?' she asked loudly.

'It seems so, dear,' Clara replied.

A tortured cry from Grace made Averil slip her arm around her mother's shaking shoulders.

'Hush, Clara.' Henry murmured in some distress. 'Don't forget, he also owed responsibility to his wife and daughter.' He cleared his throat. 'Er, can you clarify what is to happen to my sister-in-law and niece, Mr Middleton? Are they to live in the house as long as they need it? You mentioned Grace's lifetime, but what about Averil?'

Mr Middleton glanced apologetically at Averil and then faced Henry. 'The house is yours as from today, Mr Townley. Only Mrs Townley, widow of the deceased, is put under your care.' He turned back to face Averil, his face impassive through his eyes betrayed compassion. 'Miss Townley, I'm afraid your father removed your name from his will only the day before his death. I hoped he would have reconsidered his action in time but, alas, time ran out for him before he could do so.'

Averil felt a cold chill descend through her body. 'Then what is to become of me?' she said quietly. 'Am I not allowed to remain living here with my mother?' The shock of her disinheritance made her feel like bursting into tears and it was only her pride that prevented her from doing so, but for how long, she didn't know.

Mr Middleton looked kindly upon her. 'That will be up to Mr Henry Townley to decide.' He glanced from one to the other. 'I'm sure some satisfactory arrangement can be worked out. I don't think your father wished to put you out on the street, Miss Townley.'

'You'll have to work for your living like I've had to!' Liza said spitefully, making no effort to hide her delight in their changed circumstances. 'In fact, you can have my job at the shop, for I'm sure I won't need it any more.'

Averil turned to look at her in

disgust. Serving in a sweet shop all day might have suited Liza but she couldn't see herself finding enough challenge in such a job to give her any satisfaction.

'Now, hold on, our Liza,' Henry remonstrated quickly. 'I'm sure we can work out something more satisfactory than that for the lass. This is her home, after all.'

'Was her home.' Clara corrected. 'It seems to me that things have changed now. We need to give some thought before we make out the new arrangements.'

'Quite so, Mrs Townley,' Mr Middleton agreed in relief that the matter was being taken so quietly. He had not approved of his client's action but knew that he had been in sound mind, if not sound body, when he had made that sudden change to his will. 'Now, if I may finish the reading, I can leave you to discuss future arrangements.'

Averil was frozen into immobility. She was destitute and homeless. What would happen to her? Her aunt had no fondness for her, that was well known, and her cousin, Liza, would delight in their reversal of fortunes.

Her mother was openly weeping and Averil drew her closer, murmuring, 'It'll be all right, Mamma. It'll be all right.'

But she knew it wouldn't.

As soon as Mr Middleton was through the door, Aunt Clara took command. 'We may as well start as we mean to go on,' she said briskly. 'The first thing to do is to sort out the bedrooms. Henry and I shall have the master bedroom, of course, as it's only fitting.'

Averil made a movement of protest but Grace weakly raised her head, dabbing at her eyes with her handkerchief. 'It's all right, dear; really it is. I'll move in with you. We'll manage, we have to.'

'As elder daughter of the house, Liza will take over the second front room, and maybe Jessie can share with you, dear?' Clara decided next, looking to Liza for consent.

'Oh, no, Mamma. I've had enough of sharing with Jessie. You know how untidy she is.' Liza tossed her head and looked defiantly at her mother. 'No! Averil always had that room to herself, so I don't see why I shouldn't do so!'

'And can we choose ours?' Harry asked in frank wonder at his new status. 'Come on, Jessie. I'll race you upstairs. Bags I get to choose which one I want 'cos I'm older than you.'

'Then where is Mamma to sleep?' Averil demanded, laying her own rights aside for the moment.

'There are two bedrooms on the upper floor, aren't there?' Clara stated frostily. 'I'm sure you should be grateful that Joshua saw fit to make provision for your mother's welfare, though in all Christian charity, we should not have to let her starve,' she added with magnanimity.

'But, Mary Ellen sleeps in one of them.' Averil protested. 'That only leaves the one room, and it is very small.'

'Then you may choose whom you share with, Averil. Your mother, or your fellow maid. Or would you rather be out on the street?'

'Don't you think we should leave for now, Clara, dear?' Henry interrupted. 'I'm sure Grace and Averil would appreciate some time to themselves. After all, it's been a great shock to them, and there's no hurry, after all.'

'Maybe not, in your view, Henry. But I only foresee greater hardship for Grace if we let things lie.'

She intercepted a frown from her husband and drew herself up haughtily.

'Very well,' she conceded. 'We'll leave it for today. After all we have packing to see to, don't we?'

If Averil had hoped that tomorrow would bring better tidings, she was mistaken. The clock had hardly struck half-past ten when Liza bounded up the stairs and into Averil's bedroom. She paused in the doorway, glaring at Averil.

'What do you think you are doing?' she demanded.

'Liza? You're early. I didn't expect you until later. I'm sure Aunt Clara said it would be afternoon before you came.'

'It's as well I came early, then, isn't it? As I said before, what are you doing?'

'Sorting my clothes, of course.'

Averil gaped in surprise as Liza strode forward and snatched the dresses out of her hands and flung them on to the bed.

'They're mine, now, so you can keep your hands off them,' Liza cried. 'And everything else. I'll not have you stealing my things, and don't think I don't know what you've got because I do. We'll see how you like it, now the boot's on the other foot.'

Averil was shocked. 'They're my dresses, Liza!'

'They're mine now! Didn't you hear your father's will? 'The house and its contents,' it said. So this is all mine. Mamma said so.'

Averil felt the blood drain from her face, and then surge up again in a welt of fury. 'You shan't have my things. You shan't!'

She grabbed at a dress — and Liza grabbed it too. As they pulled against each other, the dress tore apart, causing both girls to lose balance. Averil recovered first. She flew at Liza and hustled her towards the door.

'Get out! Get out! You're a mean, spiteful girl and I hate you, do you hear? I hate you! And all your family. I hate the lot of you!'

8

James accelerated hard and felt the engine of his motorcar surge with power. Across the moors he sped. The wind blew through his hair, adding to the sense of recklessness that seemed to drive him forward this past week.

He had left Belmont far behind and was now crossing Rivington Moor. Even in this bright sunshine, it had a wild, bleak air, which suited his mood exactly. He laughed — not entirely with pleasure, but the sound of it did him good.

He was approaching the reservoirs and, at the last moment, swung off the road to his right and pulled on the brake with his front wheels no more than a foot from the edge of a long drop.

He had tried to forget her. Some-times, he thought he had succeeded, but only for a short time. He had escorted Honoria Blackton to a social event but had found her conversational skills to be minimal. Cecelia Hawesthorn talked too much, and Hilary Kepple had absolutely no sense of humour.

Only Averil Townley seemed to fit his expectations, but she had cut herself off from him by becoming engaged to Oliver Markham.

His clenched fist struck the centre of his steering wheel. How could she! What did she see in the man? He was sure he didn't know!

The funeral was now over. Was it too soon to seek to speak with her?

With a spark of determination he made up his mind. He would call to see her, and, this time, he wouldn't be persuaded to leave until he had spoken with Averil herself.

His heart was racing as he parked his motorcar at the kerbside in front of *Collinswood*. His heart was thumping erratically now that he was just minutes away from seeing Averil again.

It was a middle-aged woman who eventually opened the door. He presumed her to be the housekeeper. He had his card ready in his hand and now proffered it eagerly.

'Good afternoon, ma'am. I'm sorry to bother you on such a lovely day but is it possible for me to speak with Miss Townley? Miss Townley is acquainted with me,' he added with unaccustomed lack of poise. 'As you see, my name is James Rushworth and I . . . '

He was about to add words to convey his understanding about the recent bereavement that had befallen the family but another female figure crossed the hall and looked enquiringly towards the door.

For a wild, excited moment, he thought she was Averil but, as she turned fully towards him and stepped nearer, he realised his mistake. For a moment he was nonplussed, as Averil had said she was an only child.

'Who is it, Mrs Hesketh?' the girl asked sharply. 'If he's a tradesman, send him round to the kitchen door.'

As the girl was about to turn away, something about him seemed to cause her to pause and look at him more closely. He saw her eyes narrow slightly and what he could only think of as a calculating light began to gleam in them.

James was no fool. He knew he was regarded as being handsome by the ladies and was well-used to their ploys to become acquainted with him. It had, until recently, been a particular source of delight and entertainment but, at this moment, it seemed inappropriate and he controlled his facial expression with difficulty.

If this was a relation of Averil's he marvelled that Averil was so delightful. But, for the sake of his desire to speak with Averil, he smiled charmingly.

'James Rushworth at your service, ma'am. As I have just explained to Mrs Hesketh, I would like to speak with Miss Townley.'

'I am Miss Townley!'

A faint smile appeared on her face as

she spoke. It made her look supercilious and seemed out of place on so young a face.

'Miss Averil Townley,' James persisted, emphasising Averil's name.

'Oh!' She looked displeased. 'I'm afraid my cousin isn't here.' she turned sharply to the housekeeper. 'You can go back to the kitchen, Mrs Hesketh. I'll talk to our caller. Come in here, Mr, er, Rushworth, was it?'

She nodded her head towards the door of the front room to the left of the hall and swept inside the room ahead of him.

James would rather have spoken to the more open-faced housekeeper, sensing that her eyes were trying to tell him something, but he desperately wanted to find a way to contact Averil and so he reluctantly followed the girl.

As soon as they were in the room, she whirled round to face him. 'I don't know how well you know her, but I feel I must tell you that her circumstances have changed since my uncle died.'

James' heart somersaulted. 'She isn't already married, is she?' It just couldn't have happened that quickly!

'Married? Oh, you mean to Oliver Markham.' She paused thoughtfully. 'Not yet,' she said slowly, 'though, that of course, is what we are all looking forward to happening very soon. Did you want to speak to her about anything in particular? I could pass on a message to her. I'm sure Oliver wouldn't mind. Do you know him, Mr Rushworth? Or may I call you James? My name's Liza, by the way.'

She held out her hand towards him and, not wanting to appear churlish, James took hold of it, coolly nodding his head to acknowledge her name, although he had no intention of following up his acquaintance with this young lady.

'I have met Mr Markham,' he said indifferently, careful to hide his dislike of the man. 'I would prefer to speak to Miss Townley personally, if that is at all possible. Could you tell me where I might find her?'

'I'm afraid not.' She smiled in what was obviously intended to be a coquettish manner. 'That would be stretching Oliver's generosity towards you too far, don't you think!'

James pressed his lips together and inclined his head briefly. He felt he may as well take his leave but Liza had caught sight of his motorcar parked outside.

'Ooh, is that your car, James? I'd love to have a ride in it. Do say I can.'

James didn't want to prolong his time spent with Liza. She held no particular attraction for him. On the other hand, if he played along with her for a while, she might be willing to help him see Averil.

'All right, but only up and down the hill,' he offered. 'Are you sure your parents won't object? After all, you've only just met me and I haven't been introduced to them. I wouldn't want to . . .'

'Nonsense,' Liza said airily. 'They'll

make no objection. I can get them to agree to anything I want.'

★   ★   ★

Averil's shoulders sagged as she left the doctor's house. The position of receptionist/housekeeper had already been taken. Over the past few days, she had tramped around the town asking anyone and everyone if they knew of a suitable position for her. So far, her applications had been unsuccessful.

Aunt Clara had made the alternative plain. 'You either get yourself a job, Averil, and pay for your bed and board, or you work here in my house for your keep. I'll have no idle hands, I can tell you. Your circumstances have changed and the sooner you realise it, the better it will be.'

The mere thought of working full-time as a servant under Aunt Clara's rule had made Averil's decision simple. She must get a job. Hopefully, one where she could use her brain. The discussions at the NUWSS meeting had broadened her horizon and given her confidence. Women wanted the world, and the world seemed ripe for their taking.

Fired into a more optimistic frame of mind, Averil hurried up Jones Street to the library. Maybe there would be something suitable in the local paper.

She waved to Rosie Hardshaw as she passed by the desk and said, 'Good afternoon!' to Mr Perkins, pulling off her gloves as she made for her favourite place by the window in the reading room.

'Good afternoon, Mr Crowther. How's your research coming on?'

'Satisfactory, Miss Townley,' the elderly gentleman replied. He wagged his pen at her. 'If only I were young again, like you! Ah, it would be so much better. I have boxes and boxes of notes in my study at home, all of which have to be sorted and collated.'

'Can I help you in any way? I have quite a neat hand, and, what's more,

Mrs Leatherbarrow, the president of the NUWSS, has been teaching me to use a typewriter.'

Mr Crowther smiled. 'A suffragette, eh? You have the spirit for it.'

'A suffragist, actually,' Averil corrected him. 'I don't really approve of much of the needless vandalism that some women do to further the cause. The politician whose house was stoned last week is an active supporter of the suffrage movement. What sort of reasoning lies behind that?'

'So you believe in 'Words, Not Deeds'?' Mr Crowther challenged, reversing a well-known slogan of the suffragettes.

'Primarily,' Averil agreed. Her eyes twinkled mischievously. 'But I wouldn't say no to a march of protest, or chaining myself to the Prime Minister's railings if I thought it would draw attention to our claim for equal suffrage.'

He laid down his pen and regarded her seriously. 'How serious is your offer to help me complete my work? How about fifteen shillings a week, eh? Would that tempt you?'

Averil's mouth dropped open. 'Fifteen shillings?'

'If it's not enough, tell me now.'

Averil grinned at him. 'It's more than I was expecting. It would do very nicely. Are you sure, though? You don't really know me.'

'I know enough. I may be old but I'm not senile. When can you start?'

Mr Crowther spent some time quietly explaining what he hoped Averil would be able to do for him. She would be doing what she loved, working with social history.

Aglow with her success, Averil left the library soon after Mr Crowther had departed. As she hurried along Lee Lane a motorcar paused at the top of Winter Hey Lane and turned into Church Road, heading out of Horwich towards Bolton.

Averil stopped abruptly. She was too far away to recognise the driver and his passenger but she knew whose motor-car it was. It was James' . . . and his passenger was female.

Her heart sank with desolation. Even though she knew her friendship with him had irrevocably ended, she had kept alive the dream, the fantasy, that one day they would suddenly meet and realise that they still had a future together.

But, no. She mustn't keep looking backwards.

9

The following morning, Mr Crowther showed Averil into his large study that overlooked the rear garden of his mansion-sized house and indicated all his boxes of hand-written papers that were stacked on a table along one wall.

'This is where it all happens,' he said with a smile. 'My housekeeper, Mrs Baker, is banned from cleaning in here, so you may find it to be a bit dusty in places.'

Averil looked around at the array of boxes, some with lids, some without, some labelled, others not; some in fine shape, others looking about ready for the dustbin.

'I'm sure your papers could be filed better without destroying your system altogether,' she said cautiously.

Mr Crowther roared with laughter. 'Very diplomatic, my dear. I'll leave it up to you as to how you improve it. I'd like you to work out your own system for sorting everything, maybe into geographical location, historical aspects, growth of industry and suchlike. I'm afraid you'll find I haven't been too methodical myself. I write as I find.'

'What is in those other boxes over there?'

'They are photographs that my grandson is collecting for me, and taking new ones, such as Lord Lever's developments. I'll arrange for you to meet him before you get too far into the work. Two heads are better than one. Now, have you any questions?'

'Not at the moment. I'm eager to make a start.'

'Good. Take a walk in the garden whenever you feel like a breath of fresh air, and I'll send Mrs Baker in with a cup of tea or whatever you prefer.'

The time passed swiftly. She set up a new storage system and placed the new set of boxes along another table on the adjacent wall, starting with *General*

Information and going on to *Local History, as affected by National Events, Local Industries* and *Local Social Changes.*

By the end of the week, she felt she had worked there forever. She spent most of the mornings reading through sheets of notes and placing them in the appropriate boxes and then practised her typing for an hour or so on the type-writing machine that Mr Crowther had bought for the purpose.

After lunch, she resumed the reading and sorting of the notes, eager to be at the stage of beginning to type out Mr Crowther's handwritten words.

The content was of great interest to her and she often forgot that she was in paid employment, so great was her enjoyment. She was also looking forward to looking at the photographs that were in the other boxes but, so far, Mr Crowther's grandson hadn't put in an appearance.

'He'll be out and about, entertaining some young lady or other, the young whipper-snapper!' Mr Crowther complained, the twinkle in his eye belying his stern expression. 'Leaving a trail of broken hearts behind him.'

Averil smiled but forbore to comment. It was none of her business what his grandson got up to.

'Getting over what might have become an unsuitable alliance with some young lady, so his sister tells me,' Mr Crowther added whimsically.

'Unsuitable? In what way?'

Mr Crowther shrugged. 'Knowing Lucinda, the young lady was probably of a lower social class. She takes after her father.'

'Does social class matter much in this day and age?' Averil asked, thinking of her own aborted friendship with James Rushworth. He hadn't seemed to mind their different social standing at first, though her present standing was another thing altogether. Probably the fact that she was now penniless had something to do with his disappearance from her life, that and her father's disgraceful treatment of him. No wonder he hadn't been back.

'It matters to some,' Mr Crowther voiced his opinion. 'To those who don't want to be thought to be marrying 'beneath' them. Though I've no doubt it also works in reverse, you know, someone too proud to want to be thought to be after someone's money. Which way would you choose, eh, Miss Townley? Would you marry for money, or be put off from it, I wonder?'

Averil thought sadly of James. His greater wealth hadn't mattered one iota to her, and Oliver's superior opinion of his elevated social standing hadn't attracted her either.

'I would marry for love, whatever the case,' she decided firmly. 'I certainly wouldn't contemplate a loveless marriage.'

Mr Crowther nodded. 'Well said, Miss Townley! Now, enough of money or the lack of it. Let's get back to business.'

The following Monday afternoon,

Mr Crowther announced that he was travelling to Bolton Library to follow up a line of research. 'The librarian promised to get hold of some further information for me,' he explained. 'I should be back before you leave but, if not, I'll see you tomorrow.'

Averil typed another sheet. She felt pleased with her progress, both in sorting out the notes and in the actual physical task of typing.

The sound of a door banging drew her attention away from her work and she cocked her head to one side, listening for a repeat of the noise. Tucked away as this room was, she hadn't heard anyone knocking or ringing the bell. Maybe Mrs Baker was bringing a fresh jug of water?

She resumed her typing, only to be distracted once more. This time, it was a male voice, calling, 'Grandfather? Are you home?'

As Averil's gaze was drawn towards the door, it opened. Averil felt the blood leave her face and her fingers froze on the keys. Framed in the doorway was James Rushworth.

They stared at each other. It was James who spoke first. 'Miss Townley. I had no idea. When my grandfather spoke of a lady assistant, I never dreamed . . . '

Averil felt overwhelmed by James' sudden presence. How often had she imagined such a scene? They would meet, they would recognise each other and smile, they would move towards each other with a cry of delight, and everything would be all right again — but it didn't seem to be happening like that.

She was sure she had seen an initial glimmer of delight in James' eyes, but it disappeared so quickly, she felt she must have been mistaken. His expression was now cool, his eyes disinclined to hold hers and his stance stiffened.

Averil felt her poise crumble. He wasn't delighted to see her. He was embarrassed and no doubt he wished himself a million miles away. She strove to control her facial features.

'Mr Rushworth!' she said in the same tones he had used. 'I, too, am taken by surprise.' Her hands were shaking and she removed them from the keyboard and laid them in her lap where they could shake unnoticed. 'Your grandfather, Mr Crowther, hasn't referred to you by name. He merely . . . '

So unnerved was she by his unexpected presence that she knew she was in danger of gabbling nonsense, and she pressed her lips together in the hope of retaining at least some dignity.

A sudden remembrance of Mr Crowther talking about his grandson's recent escape from an 'unsuitable alliance' sent a rush of heat sweeping over her body, starting at her head and returning there after weakening every muscle and organ within her. She was that unsuitable person. He must have decided that her lack of property and expectations made her unacceptable.

'You . . . are well?' she heard James' voice ask, as all sense of light and hope died within her. 'You and your mother?'

An instinctive need to cover her shame came to her aid and she managed to control her trembling lips, although her cheeks were burning.

'Yes, indeed,' she replied quietly, her eyes avoiding his face.

'And . . . Mr Markham? He is . . . comforting you?'

Mr Markham? What on earth had Oliver Markham to do with her situation? Even as the amazement caused by the question surged through her, a tiny part of her mind grasped the name as a drowning man grasps at a straw. It was a way to save her pride from complete extinction.

'Yes,' she almost whispered. 'We are . . . very grateful to him.'

'Grateful?' his voice scorned.

A flash of annoyance jerked her head high. 'And why not?' she asked with fire in her eyes. 'He came the very minute he knew of my father's death. And he . . . ' What could she say without lying? ' . . . he offered his full support.

We were grateful indeed!'

She forced her gaze to hold his, and it was now James who looked away.

With a sinking heart he realised he had lost his chance with her, on two occasions. He should have forced his way past Oliver Markham after Joshua Townley's death. And he should have insisted on speaking with her the day after he met Liza. It might not have been too late. Both omissions were his own. He could blame no-one else.

'Then, I am . . . pleased,' he said lamely, knowing how far from the truth it was. He cleared his throat and tried to think of something to ease the tension between them. 'I didn't know you could type,' he said eventually.

'No. Well, you didn't know much about me, did you?'

Only that I love you, his heart cried.

How could he cope with seeing her whenever he called on his grandfather? How could he work closely with her as they sorted through the material and photographs for his grandfather's book, and not be able to touch her, not be able to hope that one day she might fall in love with him?

In the same instant, he knew that he couldn't turn away from that chance to be near her, but he had to give her the opportunity to refuse.

'Do you wish to continue with this?' He swept his arm around the room.

Averil felt her heart drop even further. He didn't even want her to be involved in his grandfather's work. But, why should she give up so readily. Mr Crowther liked her and was willing to work with her. He wasn't a social snob like his grandson.

With a chill, she realised he might be, if he knew of their recent friendship, but she needed this chance to better herself. It had saved her from being her aunt's servant. Why should she be the one to lose out again?

'I have promised to help your grandfather, and I enjoy it!' she added a trifle defiantly. Maybe, if she could convince him to continue to believe that Oliver was still on the scene, he would find the situation possible to deal with, and they could at least be friends and help Mr Crowther complete his manuscript.

'I see no need to tell Mr Crowther of our unfortunate ... friendship,' she said reasonably.

James nodded. Unfortunate friendship, indeed. Nothing more fortunate had ever happened to him.

'Why not?' he said cheerfully. 'Tell my grandfather I shall call again tomorrow.'

10

When James arrived on Tuesday morning, Mr Crowther introduced Averil to him and they politely shook hands. If Mr Crowther thought their attitude towards each other to be overly cool, he didn't comment on it.

After an initial awkwardness, Averil's natural interest in the local photographs shone through and she seized upon one after the other.

She was conscious of James' closeness and gently moved away from him, hoping he wouldn't notice.

He did. He was too aware of her not to do so. As she moved away, the light perfume of her hair wafted into his nostrils and he longed to reach out and touch her, to draw her close again. If his grandfather hadn't been present, he might have risked it, but was it right to seek to attract a woman engaged to be married to someone else? He knew it wasn't — but how could she prefer Markham to him?

Averil found her days to be a battle of emotions. How could she help it when she longed to melt into his arms and feel his lips upon hers?

But she kept her thoughts to herself. Mr Crowther would probably be distressed to know that she was the 'unsuitable' person James was getting over.

Averil threw herself into her suffrage activities, joining others in the evenings in the home of Mrs Leatherbarrow on Scholes Bank. There, alongside other young women, she typed letters to well-known personalities, designed posters to advertise suffrage events and delivered mountains of handbills to countless homes in Horwich.

The highlight of the week was the meeting over the co-operative shop on Lee Lane. Ordinary women came to tell of suffrage activities in other areas, women who, in less fervent times, would never have dreamed of standing up before a roomful of women who were eager to learn what more they could do to encourage the politicians to make the vote available to all over the age of twenty-one.

On this particular Thursday, Averil was taken aback by a plea from Liza to accompany her to the meeting.

'I didn't think you were interested in such matters, Liza. You will probably find it very dull.'

'No, I wouldn't. Tell her, Mamma. Averil just wants to stop me from going.' She threw a scornful look at her cousin. 'My friend, Maisie Peters, goes and she says she has a wonderful time. Do say I can go, Mamma.'

Liza had her way, and the two girls set off together.

Having Liza with her was far from Averil's choice of a good idea. She now glanced to the rear of the meeting room, where she could hear undertones of chatter and giggling. She willed Liza to look her way so that she could frown at her, but Liza was too intent upon her friend's conversation.

'Attention, ladies!' The chairlady called. 'As you all know, we are to show our support of our sisters who are on the pilgrimage to London by holding a Field Day on Saturday. Many ladies from adjoining towns will be joining us, so it will be a worthy witness.

'We are starting our programme by marching in a procession through the town and will meet by The Crown Hotel at half-past two. We will walk anticlockwise along Chorley New Road, up Winter Hey Lane to the top and along Lee Lane back to The Crown.

'Lord Lever has given us permission to set up stalls on the piece of spare land at the end of Pike Road, and I am pleased to be able to tell you that Lady Lever has agreed to open our proceedings.

'Lord and Lady Lever are due to spend Monday evening at Knowsley Hall, where I am sure you all know, our King and Queen are taking a rest from their tour of Lancashire as guests of Lord Derby. I'm sure Lady Lever will be ready to speak to his Majesty on our behalf if she gets the opportunity.

'Wear your hat badges and scarves with pride on Saturday and as long as the pilgrimage lasts. More will be on sale on Saturday, along with other handicrafts, jams, marmalades, cakes and biscuits . . . in fact, anything that will help to raise more money for our dear pilgrimage sisters.'

After the meeting was over, Averil reprimanded Liza for her behaviour. 'You're such a fuddy-duddy!' Liza laughed. 'No-one else minded. Besides, we were making plans for Saturday. It's going to be a laugh, isn't it?'

'That's not the main idea,' Averil reproved her. 'However,' she added, relenting a little, 'there's no reason why we shouldn't enjoy ourselves.'

On Friday, as Averil was about to depart for home, James detained her. 'Would you like to accompany me on a short motoring trip to Rivington tomorrow afternoon?' he asked casually. 'I am hoping to take some photographs of the animals in Lord Lever's enclosures, and of the two barns. I thought you might be interested to see my camera in action, and, maybe even be willing to pose in appropriate places for some of the photographs.'

Averil's heart leaped ... but she instantly quashed any hopes of agreeing. How could she? It would be far too intimate an outing. As for his reference to the barn, did he not remember her humiliation at the ball?

'I ... erm, have other arrangements,' she stammered. 'The NUWSS, you know, the suffrage group that I belong to, we are having a procession and a field day to raise funds for our case.'

'Ah! Yes, I remember your interest.' He cocked his head to one side and regarded her quizzically. 'Does Mr Markham support your views in that matter? I would have thought he ... '

'I make my own decisions as to what I do in my own free time,' Averil snapped hastily. 'Mr Markham . . . holds no sway over my political views.'

'Hmm. Good for you,' James approved. 'All the same, I . . . '

Averil felt turmoil within. Nothing would have been more delightful than going for a drive in his motorcar, if only her circumstances were such that such an outing were possible.

'I really must be going,' she interrupted him. 'There's such a lot to do for tomorrow, biscuits and cakes and . . . ' Her voice tailed off. She rammed her hat on to her head. 'Good afternoon, James. I'll see you on Monday.'

Saturday was bright and sunny and the main streets of the town were filled with shoppers. As the procession began, shoppers were drawn on to the streets to watch, some to cheer, some to jeer. Averil and Phoebe had volunteered to sell hat badges and so forth to the crowds, so, their trays hanging around their necks on stout ribbon, they walked among the onlookers as they lined the pavements.

To Averil's discomfort, she was suddenly confronted by the portly figure of Oliver Markham. His raised eyebrows brought a faint blush to her face.

'Really, Miss Townley, is this what you are come to?' he asked with a superior air.

Averil tossed back her head. 'Not at all, Mr Markham. This is voluntary work, for a good cause. Perhaps I can persuade you to buy a buttonhole?' She made her voice light and carefree, though she felt far from comfortable

'I don't think so,' Mr Markham declined smoothly. 'In my opinion, it's time the government strengthened its laws and banned such outrageous demonstrations as this.' A look of distaste passed over his face. 'I begin to see that I had a fortunate escape.'

'Indeed you did,' Averil replied cheerfully, regaining her mastery over the situation. 'Good-day, Mr Markham.'

Later, whilst helping to sell cakes and biscuits from the stall, she was surprised to see James approaching, carrying a large basket over his arm. He smiled charmingly at all the ladies, bringing blushes and bright eyes to many.

'An offering from Mrs Baker,' he announced, whipping off the cloth to reveal the culinary delights inside the basket. 'She is well-named, as you can see.'

'How kind, young man!' Mrs Perkins thanked him. 'Are you a supporter of our cause?'

'So-so,' he commented. 'It depends on the issue at stake. Maybe Miss Townley would care to explain when all of this is over?'

He fixed his eyes on Averil's face, delighting to see her cheeks glow with the heat of embarrassment.

Averil titled her nose in the air. 'I will be too busy tidying up afterwards,' she declared primly.

'Nonsense, Averil,' Mrs Perkins contradicted her. 'Besides, we need someone to convey our thanks to Mrs Baker. Who better than you? Come back in an hour, young man. We'll be just about finished then.'

Mrs Perkins' prediction was almost spot-on. Every last cake and biscuit was sold and the stall dismantled within the hour.

'Now, Phoebe, will you help Sarah to carry the awning over to Mrs Leather-barrow's home?' Mrs Perkins requested. 'Averil, you had better wait here with the basket. Your nice young man will expect to find you here.'

'He isn't my young man!' Averil protested.

'Isn't he? I'm sure he'd like to be.'

'No, no. Really. I work for his grandfather, that's all.'

She put the basket over her arm and with a wave of her hand, she set off to cross the road. As she glanced to her left to make sure the road was clear, she saw her cousin, Liza, and her friend, Maisie, further along Pike Road. Deciding it would be best to remind Liza that it was time she made her way home, she stayed on that side of the road and approached the two girls.

Whatever were they doing? Liza had a basket over her arm and was delving into it, offering it to Maisie to do likewise.

'Liza!' Averil called in greeting.

Liza glanced towards her, a mixture of expressions flitting over her features, dismay, hesitance, a gleam of purpose, exchanged with Maisie and finally, defiance.

To Averil's amazement, both girls drew back their arms to throw something. In the same moment she became aware that a motorcar was approaching from behind her. Thinking it might be James, she turned to look but it was a much larger vehicle belonging to someone of the upper class, she guessed. A clear view of the lady's face reinforced her guess. It was Lady Lever, who had opened their proceedings earlier that afternoon, expressing her sympathy with the ideals of their cause.

It was the expression of surprise on Lady Lever and her driver's faces that made Averil turn her gaze back to where Liza and Maisie were standing, at the exact moment when they threw their missiles, bombarding the motorcar with eggs.

Averil was shocked. The driver of the motorcar made as if to stop, but Lady Lever tapped him on the shoulder and commanded him to drive on. Liza and Maisie picked up the hems of their skirts, ran across the road and disappeared up Mary Street West.

No-one else seemed to have witnessed the incident and with a grim expression, Averil crossed the road also and followed in the wake of her cousin. She caught up with Liza and Maisie just before they arrived back on Lee Lane. The two girls were giggling together, full of excitement over their daring.

'Liza Townley. And you, Maisie Peters. You should be shamed of yourselves,' Averil exploded.

'Oh, away!' Liza retorted cheekily. 'You're such a sour puss. I bet you wouldn't dare to do such a thing.'

'I don't wish to do anything like that,' Averil retorted back. 'That was Lady Lever in that motorcar. You probably frightened her to death.'

'Serve her right.'

'How can you say that? Didn't you listen to what she was saying? Just wait 'til your parents hear.'

'I'll say you're lying,' Liza declared. 'D'you hear that, Maisie? You'll back me up, won't you?'

'Well, I . . . ' Maisie began uncertainly. 'Aren't suffragettes supposed to glory in their crimes? And get arrested and all that?'

'We'll get round to that another time,' Liza dissuaded her. 'This time, we say nothing.' She looked defiantly at Averil. 'It's two to one, so you know who'll be believed.'

Averil did know . . .

'Why do you hate me so?' Liza pouted, as Averil quietly reported her actions to Aunt Clara. 'You know how she always tries to get me into trouble,' she swiftly reminded her mother. 'She's just making it up. Ask Maisie when you next see her.'

'It's very childish of you, Averil,' Aunt Clara reproved her. 'You must apologise to Liza and then go to your room.'

'There's nothing for me to apologise for,' Averil denied. 'I have told the truth.'

She turned on her heels and strode to the door.

11

Monday began with an apology from James. 'I'm sorry I missed you yesterday,' he apologised. 'One of my tyres burst and I had to get it mended.'

He didn't add how he had agonised over whether or not to visit her at home later that evening or on Sunday afternoon. He had desisted only on account of fearing that she wasn't ready to accept that he was pursuing her affections. Plus the fact that Oliver Markham might have been present, and an unpleasant encounter wouldn't have endeared him to her.

'That's quite all right,' Averil returned airily.

She didn't add that she hadn't waited to see him, though she wasn't sure why, for, after all, she wanted to dissuade him from courting her again, didn't she? Nor did she mention the episode of the egg throwing, but she knew only too readily why that was. She was too ashamed to be so closely connected to it.

James was standing quite close to her and she caught the faint scent of pine needles. She knew it must be something he applied to his skin each morning because she had smelled it before when he was near. The fragrance tantalised her senses and she longed to breathe in deeply . . . but, instead, she turned away and began to busy her fingers with some of the papers she had typed on Friday, conscious that James was watching her.

'I'll continue with these, shall I?' she suggested nervously, wishing that James would apply to sorting through some of the, as yet unread, papers. She was totally unprepared for James to swoop his right hand upon her left wrist and pull her hand upwards to where he could clearly see her ringless fingers. He stroked the back of them with his thumb, sending tremors of awareness spiralling through Averil's body. She couldn't prevent a small gasp escaping through her lips.

'I see you don't wear an engagement ring,' he said softly.

Their eyes met briefly and Averil was sure she saw a glimmer of triumph in his gaze. She broke eye contact as she tried to jerk her wrist out of James' grasp, knowing that her cheeks were flaming with guilt.

'Er, no. I, er, don't wear it for work,' she said hastily.

'Do you ever wear it?'

'Er . . . Of course! That is . . . '

She hated lying and faced him angrily. What business was it of his whether or not she wore an engagement ring? He had no serious interest in her — since she was beneath his station in life. She felt the hurt again of Mr Crowther's phrase, 'an unsuitable alliance', and drew herself tall with wounded dignity.

'Please release my hand, Mr Rushworth,' she said coolly.

This time she steeled herself to look him straight in his eyes and hold the gaze. She watched James' eyes narrow slightly and wondered what he was thinking. However, he released her hand and had the grace to appear slightly ashamed of his action.

'I'm sorry,' he apologised. 'That was unforgivable of me. It was just . . . I saw you talking with him on Saturday and I didn't think he showed you due courtesy.'

He smiled ruefully. 'I think I hoped your . . . ' He hesitated over the next word. He couldn't bring himself to say, 'loving'. ' . . . liking of him was cooling and that we might resume to, er, walk out together, now that your father no longer . . . '

He stopped in embarrassment, realising that he had been about to speak disparagingly about her father's strict control of her.

His embarrassment and honesty softened Averil's stance against him. There was nothing she would like better than to walk out with him and for a wild, uncontrolled moment she was tempted to tell him the truth . . . that she was now penniless, with no hope of a dowry and only had a roof over her head because of her uncle's beneficence, but what would be the point?

James' class always looked for a good match, as Mr Crowther had implied in his comment. She could understand that. They had their inheritance to build up and pass on. To pursue their friendship again would only make their eventual break-up more heart rending when he felt the need to settle down and marry.

'I'm sorry,' she said, as gently as she could. 'I have no wish . . . ' Oh, the words were hard to say, but she must, ' . . . to walk out with you.'

She saw the blood drain from his cheeks and wanted to reach out and touch him, but that would be fatal to her denial. 'I'm sorry,' she repeated. 'But, surely, we can still be friends and,

and work together?' She didn't think she could bear not to see him again.

James smiled sadly. 'Yes, I expect we can.'

The atmosphere was strained throughout the day and James left early. He needed to race his motorcar over the moors and drive this ache out of his head and his heart.

He parked in his favourite spot overlooking the reservoir and switched off the engine. Leaving his car where it was, he climbed up higher and squatted on a rock, his arms clasped around his knees.

Something wasn't right. He knew Averil liked him. He hadn't lost his touch to that extent. Heavens he had spent a lifetime enjoying female adoration, even from his mother and sister, although they also knew how to cut him down to size. Was that what Averil was doing? Cutting him down to size . . . as a prelude to accepting him? Comforting though the idea might be, he somehow didn't think it was a genuine option to hope for.

No, it was something else.

He had seen the light in her eyes, and watched it grow dim, and she was lying about her ring. She hadn't got one. Oliver Markham was too mean to buy her one. He didn't deserve her, and he had a good mind to tell him so. Why, he would shower her with diamonds, given the chance. Diamonds, sapphires, rubies . . . whatever she wanted. And silks and satins.

She had been reasonably well-dressed when first he knew her. She had been in a different outfit each time he had seen her . . . and her ball gown had been delightful. So why did she always wear the same outfit for work?

Indeed, why did she need to work at all? He was sure she hadn't been at work the day he first met her — yet his grandfather paid her a wage.

Maybe he had better make a few discreet inquiries? And he could start with that little minx of her cousin. She'd told him Averil didn't live there anymore, but he knew she did. He had followed her home one afternoon.

He stroked his chin thoughtfully. Suddenly, he leaped to his feet and returned to his car more hopefully than he had left it.

The leading item on the front of *The Bolton Journal* on Monday evening was about the *disgraceful act of vandalism directed against Lady Lever after the NUWSS procession and field day on Saturday*. The reporter denigrated the act, criticising the whole of the women's suffrage movement for encouraging their members to commit such outrageous personal attacks against respected persons of society.

Averil saw it with dismay, knowing that the committee members would be making further enquiries to try to discover the perpetrators. She wondered what Aunt Clara would make of it, having chosen to disbelieve her about Liza's part in the attack.

Aunt Clara saw no reason to change her mind. 'Since you saw it happen, Averil, you must accuse the real culprits, instead of persisting in your wicked lies against dear Liza and her friend. You have always had it in for her and I really cannot condone your attitude any longer.'

'I'm sorry that I cannot oblige you, Aunt,' Averil said calmly. 'I have said all that I intend to say. I saw Liza and Maisie throw the eggs and I cannot change my story and accuse anyone else.'

'There. You heard her! It's all a story,' Liza exclaimed triumphantly, her eyes gleaming with challenge. 'Admit that you were lying.'

'I've nothing else to say,' Averil shrugged. She knew there was no point in taking her accusation anywhere else. Liza would lie her way out of it and it would cause unnecessary scandal.

Early that evening Liza announced that she was going out with Maisie. Averil suspected that she was up to something. It was the look in her eyes, Averil thought.

'Well, aren't you asking where I'm

going?' she demanded of Averil.

'If you wish to tell me,' Averil replied lightly, knowing that to demand the answer would be certain to achieve the opposite.

Liza tossed her head. 'Well, I don't . . . though I may tell you when I get back.'

'Please yourself,' Averil countered. 'I really couldn't care less.'

It was mainly true. She just hoped Liza wasn't planning more mischief under the auspices of the suffrage movement.

Remembering that King George V and Queen Mary were staying that weekend at nearby Knowsley Hall as guests of the Earl and Countess of Derby, she looked at Liza sharply. Surely Liza wouldn't be so rash as to risk making a scene there.

Averil was meeting Phoebe and they were going to Mrs Leatherbarrow's house to assist with the many tasks that needed to be done. More fund raising activities were planned and the details needed to be decided upon and the task of putting them into action delegated to the willing volunteers.

Averil was made assistant to Dolly Hilton, the correspondence secretary and her first letter was to Winston Churchill, asking him to reaffirm his support of the NUWSS, now that the Reform Bill had been withdrawn, pointing out the promise of a Private Members' Bill in the next session of parliament was mere 'straw in the wind'.

She raced home, nearly bursting with excitement. As she hurried up Church Road, she could see a motorcar just leaving the front of their house. She stopped abruptly. It was James' car. What was he doing? Had he called to see her? He hadn't said that he would.

An anxious thought struck her. Mr Crowther! Oh, surely nothing had happened to him. Oh, dear.

She resumed her hurried way up the hill, all thoughts of her suffrage activities temporarily pushed to one side and she burst into the hall. Liza was brushing her hair in front of the mirror. She didn't look particularly pleased with herself, though the pouting expression changed into wilful defiance as she faced Averil.

Averil didn't waste words on a greeting but went straight to the hub of the matter.

'Liza? That was James Rushworth in that motorcar! What did he want? Did he leave a message for me?'

The smug expression on Liza's face warned her that the answer wasn't going to please her!

'A message for you, Averil? Why should James leave a message for you? You've never said that you know him.'

Averil stared at her. It hadn't occurred to her that James might know Liza.

'But, how do you know him? Where have you met him?'

'You're not the only one who gets out and about, Averil! I've known James for . . . some time, actually. It's lovely to drive in his car. Have you been in it yet?'

No, she hadn't! And, now, it looked as though she never would. What did he see in Liza? It must be something special if he was willing to disregard her social status.

Averil was lost for words. Her mouth opened and closed but no words would come out.

Liza put down the hairbrush and patted her hair back into place. 'You look like a goldfish, Averil,' Liza said unkindly. 'Maybe I can give you some tips on how to catch a man's eye? But, some other time, eh.' Her face tightened and she swung on her heel and ran up the stairs.

Averil stared after her. Her world had suddenly fallen apart.

12

Averil wasn't especially looking forward to seeing James on Tuesday morning. She wondered if he would make mention of his outing with Liza — but he didn't.

'Did you do anything special last night?' she asked eventually.

'Not really,' James replied, shrugging his shoulders. 'And you?'

'I attended the NUWSS meeting,' she said, hoping she sounded as nonchalant as he had. 'I wrote a letter to Winston Churchill,' she added with more life in her voice.

'Threatening to throw a brick through his window, were you?'

Averil was taken aback by the coldness of his voice. 'No. Asking for his continued support, as it happens. He is on our side, you know.'

'That doesn't appear to mean much

to women like you.'

'What do you mean, 'women like me'?' she exclaimed indignantly. 'I've made no secret of my support of women's suffrage. You haven't spoken so strongly against us before.'

'I wasn't previously aware how far you would go to express your views.'

'Meaning?'

'I think you know what I mean. Let me put it this way, does the word 'eggs' mean anything to you?'

Averil gaped at him. 'Eggs?'

She knew a flush was rising up her face. He had been with Liza last night. What had Liza said about the incident?

James' eyebrow rose perceptively. 'I see you get my meaning!'

'I didn't . . . '

'Your cousin told me!'

'Oh, so you do admit seeing her behind my back?'

'Behind your back. My dear girl, don't come that one. You've had your chances.'

Averil was furious. 'Well, I obviously

made the right decision, didn't I?' she snapped.

James looked equally angry. His lips tightened. 'Obviously!'

He hesitated for a moment, then swung on his heel. 'I'm going out!'

And the door slammed behind him.

He soon discovered that Horwich was abuzz with the news that *Roynton Cottage*, the Lancashire home of Lord and Lady Lever, had been burned to the ground overnight . . . and arson, by persons unknown, was suspected. The tale lost nothing in its re-telling and, naturally, everyone's suspicions turned to the suffragette movement.

Averil first heard about it when James strode back into the room, his face dark with anger.

'Your movement has gone too far this time,' he announced without preamble.

'Pardon?'

'Lord Lever's home was set alight last night. It's completely gutted.'

Averil's hands rose to her face in shock.

'But why do you suspect the suffrage movement? Lord Lever is one of our supporters. No-one with any sense would attack him.'

'Since when did sense have anything to do with it? Remember eggs and Lady Lever?'

At the back of Averil's mind, she made the same connection, but she knew the real culprit of the 'eggs' incident. Surely Liza wouldn't have had anything to do with this? Was that what she had been planning to do?

'You know something, don't you?' James challenged her, his eyes intent on her face.

'No.'

Averil knew her tone wasn't convincing but, wanting neither to lie nor incriminate Liza, it was all she was prepared to say.

To James, her brevity spoke for itself. He swung on his heel and strode to the door.

'Where are you going?' Averil couldn't help asking. Was he going to take his suspicions to the police?

'To see if I can find out anything more,' James spoke over his shoulder. 'In the meantime, you need to decide how far you want to follow these crazy women, Averil. Otherwise, we're through.'

Averil stared at the door as it swung shut behind him. What did he mean, 'Otherwise we're through'? Weren't they 'through' already?

She sat down at the typewriter but couldn't settle to work. She kept thinking of the fire at *Roynton Cottage*, wondering how widespread it had been. Had Lord and Lady Lever been in residence at the time? Was anyone injured?

When Mr Crowther came in, just after Mrs Baker had brought the tray of morning tea, they discussed the incident.

'Shall we stop work and go up there to see what's happening?' Mr Crowther suggested. 'Where's James? Hasn't he arrived yet?'

'He arrived soon after I did,' Averil admitted. 'He said he was going to see if he could find out more about it.'

'Good! That means we'll probably see him up there. Drink up your tea and put your hat on, Miss Townley. I'm going to call a cab.'

There were many sightseers gathered on the sloping terraces of the cottage gardens but a police cordon prevented anyone not officially connected with the incident from getting too close. Information was filtering its way through and it seemed that Lord and Lady Lever had been guests of the Earl and Countess of Derby at Knowsley Hall last evening and had left in the early hours of the morning to return to Thornton Manor, their Cheshire home.

Because of their absence, no servants had been in residence, which relieved everyone greatly.

As to how the fire had started, various rumours were spreading, but the most likely one, borne out by a typewritten note discovered in a dispatch case, was that it had indeed been caused by someone who supported the suffrage cause. The note read:

Lancashire's message to the King from the women: 'Votes for women due' — Message to the King from Liverpool: 'Wake up the Government. First give us reason to be loyal — then try us'.

Also in the case was a pair of lady's grey suede gloves, one of which had been slashed across the palm and stained with blood.

Averil heard the news with dismay. This wasn't the way to obtain suffrage for all. It would do more damage than good.

Seeing Mr and Mrs Perkins amongst the onlookers standing on one of the terrace walls, she hurried over to them, anxious to discuss the rumours with them.

'It seems so,' Maud Perkins agreed sadly. 'People are connecting the incident to an explosion in a café underneath Liverpool Cotton Exchange on Saturday night. Same as here, no-one was injured but a great deal of damage was caused.'

'We don't need this kind of publicity,' Averil declared passionately, relieved that the extra bit of news seemed to exclude Liza from the incident.

'I agree, dear, but many think it is the only way to draw attention to the injustice of the discrimination against us.'

As she listened, Averil saw James coming away from the cordoned-off site. He had his photographic equipment slung over his shoulder and she raised her hand to let him know she was there. He seemed to look straight at her, and then turned away.

'Oh!'

She had temporarily forgotten that they had parted on bad terms. Upset by his rebuff, she took a step backwards.

'Careful, dear,' Mrs Perkins warned. 'It's a big drop down there.'

Too late to avoid the danger, Averil only knew that she was falling . . . and then pain and darkness.

'Ohh!'

★ ★ ★

Averil's head ached. What had happened? Why was the room spinning round? She opened her eyes but the brightness of the light made her instantly shut them again.

Her mother's voice said, 'She's coming round. Averil, dear, can you hear me?'

Averil forced her eyes open again. 'Yes, Mamma.'

Her eyes focussed on her mother's anxious face, and then slid to her surroundings. She was lying in bed, in a large room full of beds. A woman in nurse's uniform was standing by her mother's chair.

'Why am I in hospital?'

'You fell, dear. You banged your head.'

Seeing Averil's blank expression, she added. 'You were looking at the damage caused by the fire at *Roynton Cottage*.'

'Oh! Yes . . . I remember. What day is it?'

'Wednesday.'

'Oh.'

Averil closed her eyes and relapsed once more into the freedom from pain.

The next time she opened her eyes, the sun was shining again but there was no sign of her mother. Neither was there a nurse.

Her head felt better. She flexed the muscles of her legs and then her arms. She ached a little but it wasn't too unbearable. She pulled herself up a little and rested on her elbow.

The lady in the opposite bed smiled at her. 'Hello, dear. You're back with us, I see.'

Averil smiled faintly. 'Yes, I think so.'

Her mouth felt dry and she was going to ask how could she get a drink of water, when the lady opposite glanced down the ward and said, 'Oh, here's your young man again.'

'I haven't got a . . . '

A man stood at the foot of her bed with a bouquet of roses in his hands. It was James. He was smiling tentatively.

'Am I welcome?' he asked, with unaccustomed uncertainty.

Averil wasn't sure. It would depend on what he had come to say. She searched his face for signs of his inner thoughts.

Taking her silence as a 'yes', James stepped nearer and sat down on the chair beside her bed. 'I've brought these for you.'

He put the flowers down on the bed cover, still looking uncomfortable. 'I've come to apologise,' he added, raising his hopeful eyes to her face.

'Oh. What for?'

'For not trusting you. I should have known better. If you had been involved, you would have said so.'

'What made you change your mind?'

'I went to see your cousin again. I knew she must have lied to me.' He grinned mischievously. 'I still had my camera over my shoulder and I told her I'd caught the scene on camera.'

'But no-one else was there.'

His grin broadened. 'That's what she

174

said. She still tried to wriggle out of it, said she was only there to stop you, but she knew I didn't believe her. That's when she started raging on about you . . . how mean you were and always out to get her into trouble, and how stupid you were to turn down Oliver Markham's proposal of marriage.'

'Oh, you know about that?'

'I do now. You've no idea of the agony you put me through, thinking you were engaged to be married to that pompous man.'

Averil looked slightly shamefaced. 'It was the only way I could think of to keep you at a distance. You believed what my father had said, so I let you go on believing it.'

'But, why, darling? You must have known how I felt about you?'

Darling? Had she heard correctly? She faintly shook her head. It must be the throbbing in her head, she rationalised.

'How could I think anything different? You left when my father challenged you, and you didn't come back. I hoped . . . '

She paused. How could she admit that she had hoped he would come to her?

It was James' turn to look perplexed. 'But, I did come back! I spoke to Oliver Markham. He told me your father had died and that, as your fiancé, he was taking care of everything. I sent a condolence card . . . with my address, hoping you would get in touch.'

Averil shook her head. 'We didn't receive it.'

'And then, when I came again, after the funeral, I spoke to Liza. She said, or implied, that your wedding was very imminent. Why did you let me go on thinking it when I met you again at Grandfather's house? You could have told me the truth then.'

'I thought you considered me to be socially inferior,' she answered honestly, still not fully understanding where this conversation was going.

It was James' turn to be amazed.

'What made you think that? I never said so.'

'No, but your grandfather did. He said you were recovering from 'an unsuitable alliance'! I presumed he meant me. He did, didn't he?'

James pursed his lips, shaking his head. 'I certainly never thought so. What exactly did he say?'

'Just that! 'James is recovering from an unsuitable alliance'.'

James nodded slowly. 'Hmm, that sounds more like Lucinda than Grandfather, but don't worry, once she gets to know you properly, you'll get on fine.'

Averil tried to imagine meeting his family. She found James' optimism a little hard to match. 'But what will your grandfather say?'

James grinned. 'For the past week, he has been saying continually, 'You won't do any better than Miss Townley. You'd better hurry up and grab hold of her before someone else does'.'

'Has he? But, but it won't work. What

about your family? They'll disapprove of me.'

'My family doesn't yet know you, but they'll adore you, like I do. I met your mother yesterday and I think she liked me.'

He took hold of her hand and lifted it to his lips, kissing each finger in turn. 'So, what do you say, Miss Townley? Will you allow me to court you, with a view to a speedy wedding?'

The idea still seemed far out of Averil's reach. Her mind raced through all the possible objections.

'I won't give up working for women's suffrage.'

'That's fine by me, and by the way, a woman called Edith Rigby, from Preston has admitted the arson attack on *Roynton Cottage*. You're in the clear.'

Averil stiffened. 'You didn't think . . . ?'

James laughed. 'Only teasing. Of course I didn't. I love you anyway. Anything else?'

She stared at him, wide-eyed, savouring his words. 'You love me?'

James smiled fondly. 'Of course I do,

you sweet girl. Haven't I tried to tell you so countless times?'

Averil was nonplussed. 'I, I don't know!' All of her arguments were swept away. She stared at him in shock bordering on disbelief.

'I do love you,' she said, as if convincing herself that she was about to make a momentous decision.

James smiled. 'I know you do. So, how about it?'

'I won't be meek and submissive.'

James laughed. 'I should hope not. Where would the fun be?'

He gazed down at her, sensing that all the objections she could think of had been declared. 'Will this help to persuade you?'

He slowly lowered his head and tenderly touched her lips with his.

Averil felt a tremor of joy sweep through her. Her hands seemed to lift of their own accord and settled at the back of his head and neck. She drew him closer, delighting in the increased fervour of James' kiss.

'Well, Miss Townley? What do you say?'

Averil sighed in pure happiness. 'Yes,' she said simply.

She felt the tension leave his body, realising only then how unsure he had been of her answer. She smiled happily, knowing her answer was the right one.

He drew her close once more and neither of them was aware of a very satisfied old gentleman who had happened to arrive at the ward entrance at that moment.

He nodded to himself contentedly and withdrew, drawing the door closed behind him.

We do hope that you have enjoyed reading this large print book.

Did you know that all of our titles are available for purchase?

We publish a wide range of high quality large print books including:
Romances, Mysteries, Classics
General Fiction
Non Fiction and Westerns

Special interest titles available in large print are:
The Little Oxford Dictionary
Music Book, Song Book
Hymn Book, Service Book

Also available from us courtesy of Oxford University Press:
Young Readers' Dictionary
(large print edition)
Young Readers' Thesaurus
(large print edition)

For further information or a free brochure, please contact us at:
Ulverscroft Large Print Books Ltd.,
The Green, Bradgate Road, Anstey,
Leicester, LE7 7FU, England.
Tel: (00 44) **0116 236 4325**
Fax: (00 44) **0116 234 0205**

Other titles in the
Linford Romance Library:

TUDOR STAR

Sara Judge

Meg Dawlish becomes companion to Lady Penelope Rich whom she loves and admires. Her mistress, unhappily married, meets the two loves of her life — Sir Philip Sidney, and Sir Charles Blount . . . Meg partakes in the excitement of the Accession Day Tilts and visits the house of the Earl of Essex . . . When Meg falls in love she has to decide whether to leave her mistress and life at court, and follow her lover to the wilds of Shropshire.

SAY IT WITH FLOWERS

Chrissie Loveday

Daisy Jones has abandoned her hectic London life for a more peaceful existence in her old home town. Taking on a florist business is another huge gamble, but she loves it and the people she meets. Her new life brings a new love and her life looks set for happiness . . . until the complications set in. Nothing is quite what it seems and she sets off on an emotional roller coaster. Who said life in a small town is peaceful?

ENCHANTED DESERT

Isobel Scott

A strange man takes Cindy Charles from a jeweller's in London's Bond Street to the deserts of Saudi Arabia. The man, an Arab with green eyes, is Sheikh Al Adham. He is handsome with an air of mystery that the flowing robes of Arabia emphasise . . . At the first opportunity, Cindy escapes the influence of the man whom she finds so disturbing. But on reaching England she finds him impossible to forget. And then Cindy is sent on a straightforward journey, which has an unexpected meeting in store for her.

SEASON OF SECRETS

Beverley Winter

Wealthy wildlife expert Jeremy Fenner detests gold-diggers. He masquerades as a poor man while he works on a secret project to turn his land into a game park. He is intrigued when landscaper Emma Milton kindly gives him generous terms at cost to her struggling business. But Emma's cousin Antonia wants Jeremy for herself and sabotages the work. What's more, Antonia's father has secret plans to defraud Jeremy of his land . . .

PHOEBE'S CHALLENGE

Valerie Holmes

Phoebe and her younger brother Tom escape from the cotton mills that fate had left them in and, therefore, from the evil grip of Benjamin Bladderwell . . . Helped by a stranger, they make their way to the north-east coast to trace their mother's family. Little do they realise the dangers yet to befall them and how important their illusive new friend will become to them if they are to survive the evil that dogs their past.